a **MISFITZ** mystery

Two Tigers on a String

Josh Lacey was born in London. He is the eldest of seven children. He lives in London with his wife and their daughter.

He worked as a journalist, a screenwriter and a teacher before publishing his first novel for children, *A Dog Called Grk*.

You can find out more about him and his books at www.joshlacey.com.

Also by Josh Lacey

Misfitz Mysteries
The One That Got Away

Bearkeeper

Writing as Joshua Doder
The Grk Series
A Dog Called Grk
Grk and the Pelotti Gang
Grk and the Hot Dog Trail
Grk: Operation Tortoise
Grk Smells a Rat
Grk Takes Revenge

Praise for *Bearkeeper*

"A highly enjoyable read"
Guardian

"*Bearkeeper* informs as it entertains and
intrigues as it enlightens"
FT

"Boys of 9+ will love Josh Lacey's *Bearkeeper*. . .
The humour and wisdom of his tale will
win [the author] new fans"
The Times

"There is enough here to keep readers glued to
the page and to provide them with an enthralling
introduction to 17th-century England"
Books for Keeps

"A most engaging and powerfully
dramatic adventure . . . you cannot go wrong
with *Bearkeeper*. We recommend it firmly"
Bookbag

a MISFITZ mystery

Two Tigers on a String

JOSH LACEY

mlb
MARION LLOYD BOOKS

First published in the UK in 2009 by Marion Lloyd Books
An imprint of Scholastic Ltd
Euston House, 24 Eversholt Street
London, NW1 1DB, UK
Registered office: Westfield Road, Southam, Warwickshire, CV47 0RA

ISBN 9781407109787

Printed and bound in Great Britain by
CPI Bookmarque, Croydon
Papers used by Scholastic Children's Books are made from wood grown
in sustainable forests.

1 3 5 7 9 10 8 6 4 2

www.scholastic.co.uk/zone

To Tom

BEN'S FAMILY

Celia ← New Girlfriend

Martha
American
Dead

Never Actually Married

Dad
Robotanics

Divorced Ages Ago

Mum
Jennifer
Fitzroy

Married

Jeremy
Fitzroy
my stepfather

Also Divorced Ages Ago

Nina
lives in
Bristol

Dutch
my brother
no one knows
where he is

Harmony
my sister

ME

Kit Kat
the youngest

Frank
my step brother

1

There was a large sign on Ben's bedroom door. He had drawn it himself. Each word was printed in large black letters.

PRIVATE
NO ENTRANCE WITHOUT PERMISSION
Please
knock first
and wait for the voice
which invites you to enter

Ben shared the house with his mother, his stepfather, his sister and his half-sister. When he wasn't at home, he was at school, crammed into a class or a playground with hundreds of other kids. In other words: he hardly ever had a moment to himself.

His room was his sanctuary. His private space.

He didn't want to share it with anyone.

Ben cleared enough space for an extra mattress. He emptied a drawer. He stacked books on the shelves, tossed wires into boxes and kicked junk under the bed.

And he wondered what he'd done to deserve it.

Half an hour earlier, his mum had knocked on his door.

"Yes?" yelled Ben.

"It's me. Can I come in?"

"Sure."

Jennifer poked her head into the room. "Will you come downstairs? Jeremy and I want to talk to you."

"What about?"

"Come down and you'll find out."

Harmony and Kitkat were waiting on the landing. From the looks on their faces, Ben guessed they didn't know what was going on either.

They followed their mother down the stairs to the kitchen, where they found Jeremy sitting at the far end of the long wooden table. Beside him, there was a skinny boy wearing black jeans, black socks, black plimsolls, a black T-shirt and a pair of black-rimmed glasses.

Looking at the two of them, you would have guessed immediately that they were father and son. They were the same shape – tall and skinny – and they shared the same awkward, angular movements. They even had the same expression on their faces, cool and detached and amused, as if they considered themselves to be a little more intelligent than anyone else in the room.

Frank raised his right hand. "Greetings, fellow siblings."

"What are you doing here?" cried Kitkat. She darted forward and kissed her half-brother on his cheek.

"Hello, little brother," said Harmony. She put her arms round her stepbrother and gave him a hug.

"Hi," said Ben, hanging back, not wanting to hug Frank and hoping Frank wouldn't want to hug him either. To his relief, Frank looked as if there was nothing that he liked less than hugs, hugging or being hugged.

Jennifer asked them to sit down.

"I've got something to tell you," she said. "Frank has come to stay with us."

Kitkat clapped her hands together. "Hurray!"

Jennifer smiled. "Yes, of course, it's lovely that he's here. But. . ."

And then she paused as if she didn't know how to continue.

Jeremy took over. "Something rather extraordinary has happened. Yesterday morning, Frank said goodbye to his mother, just as he always does, and went to school. When he came home in the afternoon, she wasn't there. He hasn't seen her since. She seems to have disappeared."

2

Everyone started talking at once.

"Calm down," said Jeremy. "I'll answer all your questions. Just give me a chance to hear myself think."

When they were quiet, Jeremy told them what had happened earlier that evening. He explained how he had rung Frank, expecting to have an ordinary conversation about homework and computers, and learnt that Nina hadn't been seen for a day and a half.

"As soon as I heard what was going on, I left work and drove straight to Bristol. I met Frank and then rang the police. They advised me to bring him back to London. They said there was no need for him to stay in the flat. They're looking for Nina now. They seem very confident that they're going to find her. Tomorrow morning, they're coming here to talk to Frank."

Jeremy turned to Ben.

"Your brother doesn't really want to be here," he said. "He'd much rather stay at home on his own, but he's too young to do that. So he's come to stay with us. Now, as you can appreciate, this is a very unusual and difficult situation. With any luck, it won't last for more than a day or two. As soon as Nina comes home, Frank will go back to Bristol. Till that happens, I hope you won't mind sharing your room with him."

"No problem," said Ben, trying to sound as if he meant it.

Ben lived with his family at 32 Cardinal Road, one of the nicest streets in Queen's Park, a peaceful suburb of north-west London.

The house fitted them perfectly.

The top floor belonged to the children. It was like an island, detached from the rest of the kingdom. The adults went up there, of course, and checked on the inhabitants, making sure they weren't breaking any laws. But if the kids behaved – if they got up in the morning, went to bed at night and didn't make too much noise or mess – they were allowed to rule themselves.

Harmony had the biggest bedroom, Kitkat had the smallest and Ben's was in-between the two, which will tell you, if you don't already know, who was the oldest, who was the youngest and who came somewhere in the middle.

Jennifer and Jeremy had the next floor down. They shared two rooms, a big bedroom and a small study with just enough space for a desk each, squeezed between piles of paper and stacks of books and two tall grey filing cabinets.

The ground floor was occupied by a long, thin kitchen and a large sitting room. Through a pair of big glass doors at the back of the kitchen, you walked out of the house and into a lush garden with high trellis on all three sides, covered in clematis and creepers.

There was enough room in the garden for a tent. Ben would have been happy to sleep there. He wouldn't mind sleeping in his mum's study either. Or even in the sitting room.

So why couldn't Frank?

Ben knew there was no point arguing. Whether he liked it or not, he was going to have to share his bedroom with his stepbrother.

Till Frank's mum turned up.

Come back soon, thought Ben.

Please.

*

Jennifer and Jeremy carried a heavy mattress into Ben's room. They were followed by Frank with his bags, Harmony with a duvet and Kitkat with a pair of pillows.

"You're meant to knock," said Ben.

No one took any notice.

Jennifer and Jeremy made a bed for Frank, then stood back and admired what they had done.

"Perfect," said Jennifer. "Doesn't that look cosy?"

They all turned to look at Frank. He was staring at the mattress, but he didn't say anything.

Jeremy said, "Right, it's time for bed. You've got school in the morning. Kitkat, have you cleaned your teeth?"

"Hours ago."

Ben showed Frank which shelves he could have for his clothes and his books. Kitkat took him to the bathroom and told him where to put his toothbrush. Harmony fetched him a glass of water.

The children retreated to their bedrooms and climbed into bed. Jennifer and Jeremy visited each of them in turn, kissing them goodnight and switching off their lights.

Half an hour later, the house was quiet.

Just as they did every night, Jeremy and Jennifer

double-locked the front door and checked the bolts on the garden door, then went to bed.

They talked quietly for a few minutes, discussing the children and planning what to do in the morning. Then they switched off their lights and whispered, "Goodnight", "Goodnight".

They didn't have a clue what was happening one floor above them.

3

Kitkat was the first to leave her room.

She couldn't sleep. Too many thoughts were buzzing round her head. For all she knew, people might go missing every day, but this was different. This wasn't a picture on the news or a name on the radio, but someone she had actually met. Her half-brother's mother. Her father's ex-wife. A member of her family.

She wanted to know all about it.

She *needed* to know all about it.

She crept out of bed, tiptoed across the landing and knocked very gently on Ben's door. Her knuckles made so little noise that no one could possibly have heard her.

There was no answer.

She knocked again, just as quietly. Again, there was no response from the other side of the door. She turned the handle, pushed the door open, put her head into the room and whispered, "You awake?"

"Yup," replied a low voice.

"Me too," added another.

Thirty-two Cardinal Road was an old house and the floors were thin. If they spoke loudly, Jennifer and Jeremy would hear them through the floorboards and come upstairs to investigate.

Kitkat padded into the room and closed the door behind her. "I can't sleep," she said. "Can I come and talk to you?"

"What about?" said Ben.

"What do you think?" said Kitkat.

"Global warming?"

"Ha ha." Kitkat sat on the floor between Ben's bed and Frank's mattress. The only light in the room was the gloomy yellowish glare from the street lamp directly outside the window and none of them could really see the others, but it didn't seem to matter. Kitkat turned to Frank and said, "Hey, big bro."

"Hello, little sister."

"Are you OK?"

"I'm fine, thanks."

"Are you sure?"

"Yup. Why? Don't I seem OK?"

"I suppose you do," said Kitkat. "It's just. . ."

"What?"

"If my mum went missing, I'd be miserable. And you aren't."

"You needn't worry," said Frank. "I'm anxious, stressed and depressed. I just don't show it."

"That's very dangerous," said Kitkat. "If you don't express your emotions, you'll get cancer."

"Really? How do you know?"

"I saw someone talking about it on telly. When you bottle up your emotions, they stay inside you, and then you get cancer. The thing is, Frank, you should show us what you're really feeling. Deep down inside. You should open up to us. We're your closest relations in the whole wide world. If you can't trust us, who can you trust?"

"That's a very good question," said Frank. "Maybe I shouldn't trust anyone."

"You can trust us. Can't he, Ben?"

"Of course he can," said Ben.

Kitkat turned her attention back to Frank. "You see? You can trust us. OK?"

"I suppose so," said Frank.

"Good. So, what happened? Tell us everything."

"It's pretty late," said Frank. "Maybe we should talk about this tomorrow."

"I'm not tired," said Kitkat. "Anyway, if you don't tell us what happened, we can't help you."

"How are you going to help me?"

Before Kitkat could answer, the door opened and light flooded into the room. Ben, Frank and Kitkat looked at the figure who stood silhouetted in the doorway. To their relief, they realized it was only Harmony. She closed the door behind her before speaking in a whisper: "What do you think you're doing?"

"Nothing," said Kitkat.

"Talking," said Ben.

"Come and join us," said Frank.

Harmony thought for a moment, then came into the room and sat cross-legged on the floor alongside her little sister. "You should be asleep," she said. "You've got school tomorrow."

"I can't sleep," said Kitkat. "I'm too excited." She looked round at her siblings. "We're all here! The Misfitz – together at last. All for one and one for all!"

"You shouldn't be so excited," said Harmony. "We're only together because Frank's mum has disappeared."

"You don't have to worry about Frank's mum," said Kitkat. "The Misfitz are going to find her.

Aren't we?" She looked expectantly at the others, but none of them answered. Kitkat didn't care. "Frank's going to tell us what happened to his mum," she said. "Not just what Dad told us. The whole story. The truth, the whole truth and nothing but the truth. Aren't you?"

Frank shrugged his shoulders. "I suppose I could. If you really want to know."

"Yes," said Kitkat. "I really do."

"Me too," said Harmony.

"Me three," said Ben.

"OK," said Frank. He hesitated again. "Where should I start?"

Ben said, "When did you know your mum had disappeared?"

"When I came home from school."

"Then start there."

4

It was just a normal Tuesday. Up early. Eat breakfast. Rush out. Get the bus, go to school. Lessons, lunch, lessons. Then home again.

Frank walked back from the bus stop, climbed the stairs to the flat, opened the front door and called out, "Hello? Mum?"

No answer.

If she was going to be out, she usually left a note or a message on his phone, letting him know when she'd be back, but today there was nothing. She must have been too busy.

He didn't mind.

He fetched a glass of mango juice from the fridge and three chocolate biscuits from the tin in the cupboard, then retreated to his bedroom and switched on his computer.

She still wasn't back by suppertime. He lay on the sofa, watching TV and eating the rest of the biscuits. He wasn't worried. He was sure she had an excellent reason for not coming home. He watched the headlines at ten, then cleaned his teeth and put on his pyjamas. Once he was comfortably settled under his duvet, he sent a text to his mum's mobile.

Night mum.

He could have rung her and asked where she was or when she'd be back, but he didn't want to bug her. She was a grown-up. She could do what she liked. He read for half an hour, then switched off the light and drifted into a deep, dreamless sleep.

In the morning, Frank was woken by his alarm. He got dressed, then went to wake his mother. At Christmas and on her birthday, he brought her a cup of tea in bed, but on a normal weekday, he just knocked on her door and shouted till she answered. Today, there was no response. He knocked twice more, louder each time, then opened the door.

The bed was empty. He could see that it hadn't been slept in.

He went back to his own room and checked his phone. She hadn't texted back.

He wandered round the flat. There was no sign of his mum's coat, bag or keys. Nothing seemed to have been disturbed. She hadn't come home.

For the first time, he wondered whether something might have happened to her. Even when she had a boyfriend, his mum was careful to tell him where she was going and when she would be back.

He thought about ringing her office or the police, but decided not to bother. He didn't want to cause any trouble. She must have stayed with a friend and forgotten to ring him. It had never happened before, but there's a first time for everything.

Frank was perfectly capable of looking after himself. His mum knew that. If she wanted to take a night off, he didn't mind.

He ate a piece of toast with honey and drank a glass of milk, then cleaned his teeth and packed his bag.

At school, he didn't tell anyone what had happened.

It was another ordinary day. Lessons were boring. Lunch was disgusting. At chess club, he won twice.

In the afternoon, he took the bus home. When he got back to the flat, he looked in every room just to confirm what he already knew. No one had been there since the morning. For the second night running, he was alone.

Some kids would have panicked. Others would have gone wild. Frank watered the plants.

His mum had taught him how to look after them. The pink orchid, the miniature lemon tree, the cactus in the bathroom, the pot of basil on the kitchen window sill – they and all the others required individual treatment.

Plants are like people, Nina always said. Each one is different. You have to nurture them according to their needs. Some prefer to be ignored for weeks, sucking the last drops of water from the soil, asking for nothing, happy doing their own thing. Others demand daily love and attention. She wiped their leaves and sometimes even talked to them. Frank couldn't bring himself to do that, but he watered all the ones that needed watering.

Tending to the plants took twenty minutes. When Frank had finished, he poured out the last drops of mango juice, tossed the carton in the bin and sat on the sofa, watching TV and sending some emails.

Just after six, the phone rang.

Frank snatched it up. "Hello?"

"Hi, Frank," said a man's voice.

"Oh, hi." Frank could hear the disappointment in his own voice. He wondered if his dad could too.

They talked for a few minutes, discussing school and homework, then Jeremy said, "Can I have a word with your mother?"

"She's not here," said Frank.

"Where is she?"

"I don't know."

"Is she still at work?"

"Maybe."

"Oh. OK. When will she be back?"

"I don't know."

"She didn't tell you?"

"No."

"That's odd. When did you talk to her?"

"Yesterday."

"*Yesterday?* But. . . Where is she?"

"I just told you," said Frank. "I don't know."

A little more than two hours later, the doorbell rang. Frank looked at the small square screen which showed whoever was standing at the outer door downstairs. He saw a tiny black-and-white image of his father's face, peering upwards, staring at the camera.

Frank pressed the buzzer and opened the front door. A moment later, his father came bounding up the stairs.

Jeremy stood on the landing for a second, catching his breath, then smiled awkwardly at his son. "Hello, Frank. How are you?"

"Fine," said Frank.

"Good. Great. It's nice to see you. I don't suppose she's back?"

"No."

"She hasn't called?"

"No."

"Can I come in?"

"Sure." Frank stepped aside and let his father into the flat.

Jeremy paced quickly through the rooms. Frank followed him round the flat, wondering what he was looking for.

Jeremy said, "She hasn't done this before, has she?"

"No."

"Never?"

"No."

"I thought not." Jeremy pulled his phone from his pocket and dialled 999. He asked to be put through to the police. "I'd like to report a missing person."

5

"We drove here," finished Frank. He had been talking for a long time and his voice was hoarse. The others had sat in silence, letting Frank remember at his pace, only interrupting very occasionally to ask a question. "Dad carried my bags from the car to the house. I followed him in. Your mum was waiting for us in the kitchen. She gave me a drink and a cheese and pickle sandwich. We talked for a bit. Then she came upstairs and got you." He shrugged his shoulders. "There's nothing more to tell. You know the rest. You were there."

Kitkat said, "So where do you think your mum is?"

"I don't know."

"You must have some idea."

"I don't."

"If you were the police, and you were in charge of finding her, where would you look first?"

"I've just told you," snapped Frank. "I don't know."

"I'm sorry," said Kitkat. "I didn't mean to be annoying. Are you cross with me?"

"Forget it," said Frank.

Kitkat bit her lip. Frank stared at the floor.

It was Harmony who finally broke the silence. "What's the time?"

Ben glanced at the clock on his bedside table. "Ten past two."

"That's so late. We should all go to bed."

"I'm not tired," said Kitkat. As she spoke, her mouth stretched open in an enormous yawn, as if her body was denying what she had just said.

The others yawned too. They couldn't help themselves. Yawning is contagious – especially at ten past two in the morning when you've been up since seven the day before.

"Our brains will work better when we've slept," said Harmony. "Let's talk again tomorrow. Come on, Kitkat. Time for bed."

Kitkat and Harmony tiptoed back to their own rooms. When they had gone, Ben and Frank whispered "goodnight" to one another.

And the house was quiet.

6

"If x plus 2y equals 23," said Mr Prentice, "and 3x plus y equals 19, then what is x and what is y?"

He looked around the class, waiting for someone to raise their hand.

"Can't anyone tell me? Anyone?"

The room was silent.

"Come on," said Mr Prentice. "It's not difficult. How about you, Ben?"

"No, sir."

"Have a guess."

"I don't know, sir."

"If you were going to work it out, how would you start?"

"I really don't know, sir."

"We've been studying this for three weeks now. You've been in every one of my lessons. Don't you have any idea what to do?"

"No, sir."

Mr Prentice sighed. "How about someone else? Ah, Suresh, I thought you might be able to help us. Why don't you tell Ben what to do?"

"X is 3," said Suresh. "Y is 10."

"Very good. And how do you know that?"

While Suresh explained how he had solved the equation, Ben tried to look as if he was listening, but he was really thinking about missing mothers.

He wondered how he would feel if his own mum disappeared.

If he came home from school and she wasn't there.

In some ways, he was sure, it would be an enormous relief. Without his mother bossing him around, telling him what to do and where to go, life would suddenly become so much easier. No one would nag him to get out of bed in the morning. No one would order him to change his T-shirt or put his plate in the sink. Broccoli would not pass his lips. Never again would he eat lentil soup. He could go to bed whenever he wanted – and he wouldn't even have to clean his teeth.

His existence would be one long holiday. For a few days. And then. . .

He couldn't imagine it.

However hard he tried, he just couldn't imagine what life would be like without his mum.

He wondered how Frank was feeling.

It was pretty well impossible to tell. Frank probably had feelings. Most people do. But he didn't show them to anyone else.

Frank was a strange boy. If you met him, you wouldn't be sure if he was ill or rude or both. People often thought he was autistic, but he wasn't. He'd been tested. He didn't have autism or Asperger's or anything else. He was just Frank.

Frank the freak.

That was what Ben used to call him.

And then, last summer, when they all stayed in Quarryman's Cottage, he realized that Frank was actually quite interesting.

Strange, yes. Quiet and solitary, yes. Grumpy and irritating, yes. But also clever and cunning and resourceful and a very useful person to have around if you were trying to find a missing monkey.

What about Frank's mother?

Ben didn't know very much about her.

Her name was Nina Fitzroy. He hadn't met her often, but he could remember her well. Before Frank was old enough to travel on a train alone, Nina and Jeremy would take turns to chaperone him from Bristol to London and back again. Whenever Nina dropped him off at Cardinal Road, she would stay for half an hour, sitting cross-legged on the floor, cradling a cup of herbal tea in her hands and talking in a soft voice about star signs or yoga positions or the friends that she'd made on her last trip to India.

She was a tall, thin woman with black hair and big eyes. She often touched the person she was talking to, letting her long fingers rest on their shoulder or their upper arm. She wore hippy clothes. Her hair was messy. She had a scar on her nose where it had been pierced. She taught yoga and, if you asked her nicely, she'd show you how to twist your body into extraordinary shapes.

Ben had a vivid memory of visiting their flat. The windows were wide open, but the air still stank of incense. Colourful ethnic carpets hung on the walls alongside photographs that Nina had taken in Africa and India. There were books and plants everywhere. Unwashed plates and glasses were stacked in the sink.

Just like her home, Nina was chaotic and disorganized. She never seemed to know what day it was and always arrived late for any appointment.

But why would she walk out of her front door on an ordinary morning and never come back?

What had happened to her?

Where had she gone?

Maybe she'd just had enough of Frank and decided to start a new life without him.

I could understand that, thought Ben. If I had to live with Frank, I'd probably want to run away too.

Then he remembered that he *did* have to live with Frank.

His space had been invaded. His privacy had been taken away. He no longer had anywhere to call his own.

What would happen if Nina never came back? Would Frank go back to Bristol and live alone? Would he be sent to live with foster parents? Or would he stay in London for the rest of his life, sleeping in a bedroom that didn't belong to him?

"Ben?"

He looked up.

Mr Prentice was staring at him. So were the other kids in the class.

"Did you hear what I just said?" asked Mr Prentice.

"Not exactly," said Ben.

Some people giggled, but Mr Prentice didn't look amused.

"'Not exactly,'" repeated Mr Prentice. "And what *exactly* is that supposed to mean?"

"I suppose it means 'no'," said Ben.

"Thank you for your honesty," said Mr Prentice. "I shall repeat the question. This time, I would be grateful if you actually listened. Do you think you might be able to do that?"

"Yes, sir," said Ben.

7

That night, Frank cooked omelettes.

He had been at home all day with Jeremy. In the morning, they talked to the police. In the afternoon, they went to Salusbury Road and bought three books, a cashmere scarf and food for supper.

The others sat in the kitchen and watched Frank whisk eggs in a bowl and lay out the ingredients on a wooden board: a lump of Gruyère, six slices of ham, a tomato, a red pepper, a crisp French loaf. He used two frying pans and fifteen eggs.

When the omelettes were bubbling in the pans, Harmony stirred a salad dressing, Kitkat laid the table and Ben ran upstairs to fetch the adults.

Frank's omelettes were delicious.

"This is divine," said Kitkat.

"Ten out of ten," said Harmony.

"The best omelette I've ever eaten in my life,"

said Jennifer. "And I've eaten a lot of omelettes. When I lived in Paris, I was going through a vegetarian phase, and there are only two foods that Parisians give to vegetarians. Omelettes and ratatouille. I got so sick of them, I thought I'd never want to eat another omelette in my life. But this is fabulous, Frank. You're a real chef. You should work in a restaurant."

"I would," said Frank. "If I could find a restaurant where they only serve omelettes."

When they had cleaned their plates and started on the salad, Ben quizzed his mother and his stepfather about Nina. He asked how they were planning to discover where she had gone.

"We're not planning to do anything," replied Jennifer.

"Why not?"

"Because there's nothing we can do."

Jeremy said, "The police have promised to tell us as soon as they find anything. Till then, we just have to be patient."

Ben asked more questions, but Jennifer and Jeremy refused to answer any.

"Leave it to the professionals," said Jeremy. "They know what they're doing."

*

Later, upstairs, the Misfitz assembled in the boys' bedroom and Frank told them what the police had said.

Jeremy had taken the day off work to meet them. He and Frank sat around the kitchen table with the police, drinking tea and eating flapjacks and answering their questions.

There were two of them. Detective Inspector Gareth McMillan was a tall, good-looking man with a firm handshake and a deep voice. Detective Sergeant Claire Coleridge had a warm smile and bright red cheeks as if she'd been walking briskly on a cold day. "Please call me Claire," she said. "We don't want to be too formal, do we?"

McMillan and Coleridge asked Frank to tell them exactly what had happened over the past couple of days. They wanted to know when he had last seen his mother, what she had been wearing and whether she had behaved strangely. Did anything seem different? Did she say anything unusual?

"Not as far as I can remember," said Frank.

The police had all sorts of questions about Nina's life. They wanted to know the names of her friends and colleagues. Her hobbies. Her ambitions. Her previous addresses. They asked for every detail of her education, her employment history and her medical records. They asked if she was prone to depression, anxiety, rage or sudden mood swings. Did she smoke, drink or take drugs? Did she have lovers? Or enemies? Had anyone threatened her? Had she seemed different in the past few days or weeks?

Frank could answer most of the questions. Jeremy confessed that he didn't know much about his ex-wife and he had forgotten most of what he had known.

When the police had heard enough, they told Frank and Jeremy what they had learnt from their colleagues in Bristol. Earlier that morning, two officers had borrowed a key from a downstairs neighbour and entered the flat. They searched the rooms and discovered that a few significant items were missing. There was no sign of Nina's purse, phone, driver's licence, credit cards or passport. In the cupboard and the chest of drawers in her bedroom, there were gaps where clothes seemed to have been removed.

The police were now checking hospitals, train stations, ports and airports. If they didn't find any trace of Nina in the next day or two, they would widen the search across the country and then across Europe.

"They'll find her," said Frank. His tone suggested that he didn't want anyone to disagree with him. "Wherever she is, whatever might have happened to her, the police are going to find her."

8

On Thursday, Frank stayed at home again while the others went to school. Ben wished he could stay at home too. Playing games and reading books would have been much better than going to lessons. In fact, just about anything would have been better than another day of maths, geography, English and French. But he didn't try to argue with his mother or his stepfather. He knew he couldn't win.

The three of them took the bus together. Ben and Harmony delivered Kitkat to the gates of her school, then walked to King Henry's.

At lunch, Ben sat alone in the canteen with a tuna and cucumber baguette and thought about his bedroom. It wasn't even *his* bedroom any more. It was *theirs*. His and Frank's. And while he was sitting at school, bored out of his mind by a bunch of dumb teachers, his stepbrother might be doing anything. Searching through Ben's possessions.

Trying on his clothes. Bending the spines of his books. Opening his computer. Playing his games. Reading his emails. Trespassing on his privacy.

He wanted to tell his brother to find somewhere else to sleep. Stay with a friend. Find a hotel. Just get out of my room and leave me alone.

He knew there was no point. Only one thing was going to get his room back again. The return of Nina.

But what if she never came home?

I've got to find her, thought Ben.

Frank was wrong. The police would never find Nina Fitzroy.

Yes, sure, they said they were looking for her, but they had a million other cases to solve. Cases which were much more important to them than a woman who walked out of her house and didn't come back. They had to catch terrorists with ticking bombs. And murderers. And drug dealers. And all kinds of other violent villains and dangerous criminals. They wouldn't waste much time on one missing woman.

It's up to me, thought Ben. Kitkat will want to help. Harmony might too. Maybe even Frank will. But basically it's up to me.

How do you find someone who has disappeared?

You look for them.

But how?

And where?

Ben pulled a pen from his pocket, tore a blank sheet from the back of his diary and wrote down all the questions that needed to be answered. He wrote slowly and carefully, crossing out words and rewriting sentences, trying to be as accurate as possible. He didn't want to leave any room for mistakes or misunderstandings.

Suresh stopped beside him and said they were playing football in the yard. Did he want to join them? Ben covered the page with his arm and said no, not now, he was busy. When Suresh had gone, he read through his notes, correcting what he had written.

In the afternoon, Ben sat at the back of the class, out of sight, and scribbled more notes in the back of his diary.

He tried to imagine what he would do if he wanted to disappear. Then he wondered how he would make someone else disappear.

He remembered what Frank had said and the questions that he'd been asked by the police. Remembering books and movies, he thought about the methods used by private detectives.

If he was a detective who had been hired to find a missing woman, what would he do? Where would he go? And what questions would he ask? By the end of the day, he had made a list.

9

THE MOTIVE

Why did Nina disappear?

EITHER
she wanted to
OR
someone made her.

REASONS

Did she have any reason to disappear?
Did anyone else have any reason to make her
    disappear?

THE SUSPECTS

Who?

IF NINA CHOSE TO DISAPPEAR
then the only suspect is Nina.

Before her disappearance, did she behave
   suspiciously?
Did she buy a ticket to anywhere?
Did she take her passport?
Did she mention travel or journeys?

IF SOMEONE FORCED HER TO DISAPPEAR
then who are the SUSPECTS?

Why would anyone want her to disappear?
Does she have any ENEMIES?
Did she get threatening phone calls? Or emails?
   Or letters?
Did anyone want to hurt her?

OTHER QUESTIONS

WHEN did she disappear?

WHERE was the last place that she was seen?

WHO was the last person to see her?

10

"I don't know," said Frank. He lifted his head from the list, looked at the others and shook his head. "These are all good questions, but I don't know any of the answers."

Ben, Harmony, Frank and Kitkat were sitting in the garden. It was six o'clock on Friday evening. Jeremy was still at the hospital and Jennifer was in her study, applying the finishing touches to the final draft of her book. *The Unclear Family* was almost finished. By the middle of next year, the whole world would be able to read about the difference between nuclear families and unclear families. The publishers were confident that the book was going to be a best-seller. If it was, Jennifer had promised to take the children on safari.

While Jennifer sat upstairs at her desk, the younger generation were supposed to be sitting quietly in the garden and doing their homework, but they weren't interested in reading a scene from *Romeo and Juliet* or drawing the interior of a lung. They had much more important things to worry about.

"I don't believe it," said Ben. "Read through the questions again. You must be able to answer some of them."

"It's pointless," said Frank. "The police asked half these questions. I've already told them what I know. Why do you want me to answer them again?"

"Let's just try anyway. We might learn something new."

"Like what?"

"I don't know. Answer the questions. Maybe we'll find something which leads us to your mum."

"No, we won't." Frank sighed. "Look, let's be honest, we're just a bunch of kids. Do you really think we can do better than the police?"

"Yes."

"Oh, come on."

"We can try."

"There's no point. The police can go anywhere and do anything. They have thousands of officers, covering the whole country. They have access to enormous databases of DNA and fingerprints and number plates and surveillance cameras. And if, with all this, they can't find my mum, then there is absolutely no way that four kids can."

Ben said, "The police might have all those resources, but they haven't found her, have they?"

"Not yet," said Frank. "But they will."

"What if they don't?"

"They will."

"You seem very confident."

"The police know what they're doing," said Frank. "They'll find her. If they don't, then no one will. We certainly can't."

"Why not?" said Kitkat.

"Take a look at yourself," said Frank. "Are you James Bond?"

"No, he's a boy. I'm a girl."

"Do you have a gun?"

"No."

"Or any useful gadgets?"

"No."

"Can you even drive?"

"No."

"So how are you planning to find my mum?"

"I'm not going to find her on my own," said Kitkat. "We're going to do it together. We're the Misfitz. All for one and one for all!"

"It's a nice name," said Frank. "But what are you actually going to do? How do you think you're going to find a missing person?"

"By answering these questions," said Ben, holding up his list.

Frank sighed. "Look, I know you want to help. That's great. Thanks. I appreciate it, I really do. You're being very nice about the whole thing. But I'm pretty sure I know what's happened to my mum and I can't see much point looking for her."

Ben said, "What do you think has happened to her?"

"I think she's dead," said Frank.

For a moment, no one spoke. Ben and Harmony and Kitkat stared at their brother, wondering if he could be serious. Was he teasing them? Was he fooling around? He didn't seem to be. But if he really believed his mother was dead, how could he stay so calm?

Harmony was the first to speak. "You shouldn't give up hope, Frank. You don't know she's dead."

"I didn't say I know she's dead," said Frank. "I said I *think* she's dead. It's the most likely explanation."

"Why?" asked Ben.

"She's a woman. She's gone missing. She's not a

drunk or a drug addict. If she'd had an accident, she would have been found. So she's probably been murdered."

"Oh," gasped Kitkat. "That's horrible."

"It's just reality," said Frank. "Women are murdered all the time. Don't you watch the news? The murderer will have dumped her in a canal or buried her in a shallow grave in some woods. She'll be discovered in a few days by someone walking their dog."

"You are a strange person," said Kitkat. "Do you know that?"

"I have been told that before. But I don't think I'm stranger than anyone else. I'm just more honest."

"You're stranger than me," said Kitkat.

"Maybe," said Frank. "Or maybe not."

"You don't know she's been murdered," said Ben. "You're just leaping to conclusions. Anything could have happened to her."

"I agree," said Frank. "There are an almost infinite number of explanations for her disappearance. Some are improbable. Others are almost impossible. And, of them all, the most likely is that she's dead."

"You see?" said Kitkat. "You're being strange again. You sound as if you're talking about the weather. Aren't you worried? Aren't you scared?"

"I'm just being rational."

"How can you be so rational about your own mum?"

"I try to be rational about everything," said Frank. "That's just the way I am."

11

On Monday morning, Jennifer drove all four children to school.

Jeremy had arranged for Frank to be given a temporary place at King Henry's with Ben and Harmony. He would join the classes for a few days. He met the headmaster, who officially welcomed him to the school and promised that everyone would do their best to make him feel at home.

You weren't allowed to use phones at school, but Frank took his anyway. If one of the teachers caught him, he could just pretend he didn't know the rules.

He switched it on at lunch time and discovered that he had one message.

"Hi, Frank. It's Dad. I've just spoken to the police. They said there's been a significant new development in the case. I don't know exactly what that means and they wouldn't tell me, but they're going to come round to the house this evening and talk to us. They should be here at six. Call me if you can. Otherwise I'll just see you at home. Can you tell the others? See you later. Lots of love. Bye."

A significant new development.

What did that mean?

What was a *development*? And why was it *significant*?

Had Nina been found? Was she alive or dead?

If she was alive, wouldn't they have said so?

Yes.

So she had to be dead.

They just didn't want to give the news by phone.

Was she now lying on a slab in a mortuary, just like the bodies that he'd seen on a thousand movies and cop shows?

She had to be.

There was no other explanation.

Frank rang his father, but got his voicemail. He left a message, promising to be home before six and asking if the police had given any more information, then went to find Ben.

12

Detective Inspector Gareth McMillan and Detective Sergeant Claire Coleridge arrived at twenty past six. If they were surprised to see so many people crowded round the kitchen table, they disguised it well. They had come at such short notice, they explained, because they wished to report a dramatic development in the case of Nina Fitzroy.

"We got a call this morning from our colleagues in Bristol," explained McMillan. "They had been contacted by. . ." He looked at his notes. "A man named Christian Kimmel."

"He lives on the ground floor of our house," said Frank. "He's German."

"That's right. Mr Kimmel knew about your mother's disappearance, of course. Our colleagues had already spoken to him."

"What's he done?" said Frank.

"He's been very helpful to us," said McMillan.

"When he went through the post this morning, sorting out the letters for the three flats in the building, he found something which he knew must be important. He rang us immediately."

"What did he find?" demanded Frank.

"A postcard addressed to you." McMillan opened a brown folder and took out two sheets of paper. "It's from your mother."

Everyone started talking at once. There were cries of "She's safe!" and "This is wonderful!" and "Fantastic!" Jeremy asked where she was. Jennifer asked how she was. Ben asked when she was coming back again.

Only one person wasn't smiling or shouting or joining in with the general excitement. That was Frank. In a low, calm voice, he said, "Could I see the postcard, please?"

"Of course you can." McMillan slid the two papers across the table to Frank. "These are scans of the front and back. The original is being tested at the moment in our labs, but I can tell you already that the postcard was almost certainly manufactured in India. There's a particular quality to the card, apparently, which you don't find on a European postcard."

The others crowded round and peered over Frank's shoulder.

The front of the postcard was decorated with a painting of an Indian god. He had chubby cheeks and a radiant smile and bright, fiery eyes, burning with passion. Bare feet peeked out from the bottom of his long yellow robe. He had six arms, three on each side of his body. There was a long black cord hanging around his neck, reaching down as far as his belly button, strung with two small, round, brown gems.

Ben wondered whether he had ever seen this particular picture before. He'd certainly seen others very like it. At school, they were always doing stuff about different religions. Unfortunately, he daydreamed through those lessons, just as he daydreamed through all his other lessons, so he had no idea who this god might be.

The card was addressed to Frank Fitzroy.

Darling Frank
India is wonderful. I've met a good bunch of
people. Next time, you'll have to come with
me. I miss you!
Lots and lots and lots of love from Mum.

"We just have to check a few things," said McMillan. "Frank, can you confirm that this is your mother's handwriting?"

51

"Yes."

"Are you sure?"

"Yes. But it doesn't make sense. Why would she go to India without telling me? She didn't even leave a note."

"Maybe she was in a hurry," said Kitkat.

"No way. And I'll tell you something else that doesn't make sense. This has an English stamp."

Frank was right: the card had an ordinary English first class stamp, decorated with a plain silhouette of the queen's head.

"Full marks for observation," said McMillan. "You'd make a good detective. Have a closer look. You'll see that the card was posted on Saturday and the postmark says 'Taunton'."

"Where's Taunton?" asked Ben.

Frank said, "It's a city about an hour away from Bristol." He turned to the police. "Are you looking for her there?"

"Let me give you a tip about postmarks," said McMillan. "They can be misleading. Taunton is the main sorting office for the whole region. This postcard could have been posted anywhere in the south-west."

"The postmark doesn't really prove anything,"

added Coleridge. "She could easily have met someone who was flying back to England."

"The Indian postal service is famously slow," added McMillan. "If I wanted to send a postcard from India, I'd give it to someone who was on their way back to England and ask them to post it when they got here."

Coleridge said, "She has been to India before, hasn't she?"

Frank nodded. "At least ten times. Maybe twenty."

"When was she last there?"

"In the summer."

"Where were you?"

"Staying with these guys."

"How did your mum spend her time in India? Was she travelling around the country?"

"No. Not really. She travelled a bit, but mostly she stayed in an ashram."

Ben said, "What's an ashram?"

"It's like a retreat," said Frank. "You can go there and do yoga. Or you can spend the whole day praying and chanting. I went to one with Mum about three years ago."

"That must be it," said Ben. "I bet she's gone back there."

"She wouldn't," said Frank. "Not without telling me."

McMillan leaned forward. "Do you have the details of this ashram? The name, the address? Can you tell us where it is?"

"Sure," said Frank. "I'll be back in a minute."

He pushed back his chair and ran upstairs.

Five minutes later, Frank was back, carrying his computer.

"I rang the ashram," he said. "She's not there. They haven't seen her."

"They might be lying," said Ben.

"They're not."

"How do you know?" said Harmony.

"They're very religious people. They would never lie about something like this. Actually, I don't think they'd ever lie about anything. They're just about the best people I've ever met. I spoke to the swami. He's the head of the ashram. He remembered my mum. And me too. He's going to ring other ashrams and ask around. He knows everyone. If she's really in India, he'll find her."

"India is a big place," said Coleridge. "More than a billion people live there. Does the swami know them all?"

"Most of them," said Frank. "He's a very well-connected guy."

McMillan said, "Could we have the details of the ashram? We'd like to have a chat with the swami too. If you don't mind."

"Why would I mind?" Frank put his computer on the table and turned the screen to face the police. Coleridge copied down the address and phone number in a small notebook.

McMillan said, "Did your mother have any friends in the ashram?"

"Lots," said Frank. "She makes friends everywhere. She's always talking to people."

"Was there anyone special? A boyfriend, perhaps?"

"No," said Frank.

"Or anyone who seemed especially close to her?"

"No."

"Did she talk about going back there?"

"All the time. She loved the ashram. We were going to go there together at Christmas."

"Perhaps she decided to go a little early," said McMillan.

"She wouldn't do that," said Frank. "She wouldn't run away. My mum's not like that."

"Of course not," said Coleridge.

"We're not saying she is," said McMillan.

But as they continued with their questions, it became obvious that that was exactly what they were saying. As far as the police were concerned, the mystery had been solved.

13

When the police had gone, Jennifer heated up some macaroni cheese for supper, Harmony whisked together a salad dressing, Kitkat laid the table, and Frank and Jeremy had an argument.

They were discussing what the police had said. Jeremy remembered an incident from his first marriage; Nina had gone out to see a friend for tea and not come home for three days.

"We were young then," said Jeremy. "We didn't have children. Things like that happened. I was worried. Of course I was. But Nina is that type of person."

"She's not an idiot," said Frank.

"I didn't say she was. She's different to most people, that's all. She has her own values. Her own way of doing things."

"You mean she'd abandon her own son and catch a plane to India?"

"She might," said Jeremy.

"I know her," said Frank. "I can tell you, she'd never do anything like that."

"I know her too," said Jeremy. "I was married to her, remember? Maybe I've seen a side of her that you haven't."

"You think she's in India?"

"She might be. That's all I'm saying."

Frank looked at his father for a moment. Then he shrugged his shoulders. "Fine."

And that was that. Frank refused to say another word about his mother or anything else. He ate supper in silence. If anyone spoke to him, he pretended he hadn't heard them.

The police left the scans behind. Ben pored over them, trying to tease any hidden significance from the postcard. What was Nina really saying? Was she sending a cry for help? Or giving her location?

darling frank india is wonderful i've met a good bunch of people next time you'll have to come with me i miss you lots and lots and lots of love from mum.

He puzzled over the picture on the front. He inspected the stamp and the postmark. He read Nina's words again and again, searching for anagrams or hidden sequences. He read the text from left to right and right to left, horizontally and vertically, forwards and backwards. He copied down the first letter of each word:

dfiiwimagbopntyhtcwmimylalalolfm

He divided the sequence into shorter chunks:

dfi i wim a gbop nt yht cwm im yla la lo lfm

He shifted each letter one place forward in the alphabet:

egjjxjnbhcpqouziudxnjnzmbmbmpmgn

Then one place back:

cehhvhlzfanomsxgsbvlhlxkzkzknkel

He spent supper staring at the postcard, searching for hidden messages.

But he couldn't crack its code.

14

After supper, the Misfitz met in the boys' bedroom.

"I don't like saying sorry to anyone," said Frank. "But I'm going to say it now. I am very, very sorry. You were right and I was wrong. The police are hopeless. They're never going to find my mum. We're going to have to do it ourselves."

"We can't go to India," said Kitkat.

"We don't have to," said Frank. "She's not in India."

"How do you know?"

"Because I know my mum."

"Maybe you don't know her as well as you think," said Harmony.

"You might be right," said Frank. "My mum might have been lying to me for all these years and in fact she's someone completely different. She's not my mum at all."

"I'm not saying that," said Harmony. "I'm just

saying she might not always behave how you expect. People do crazy things."

"I know they do," said Frank. "My mum does too. I'm always trying to persuade her to be more sensible. A couple of weeks ago, she went to a palm reader. She believes in astrology and crystals. She thinks homeopathy and aromatherapy are better than real medicine. She won't walk under ladders and she crosses the road to avoid a black cat. But that doesn't mean she'd run away from home and jump on a plane and fly to India. She might be crazy, but she's not mad."

"Maybe she's been kidnapped," said Kitkat.

"How can you kidnap someone and take them to India? How would you get them on the plane?"

Harmony said, "She might have been drugged."

"Airports are full of police. They'd notice something wrong. They're trained to look out for people on drugs." Frank shook his head. "She's not in India. Something's happened to her. We've got to find out what. There's only one problem. I don't know where to start."

"I do," said Ben.

He jumped off his bed and grabbed a piece of paper from his desk. Luckily, he hadn't thrown it away. He read from the top: "Why did Nina disappear? Did she have any reason to disappear? Did anyone else have any reason to make her disappear?"

"We've already been through these," said Frank. "I told you before, I don't know any of the answers."

"It's worth trying again," said Ben. "Isn't it?"

"I guess."

"Let's do it." Ben read the next item from the list. "Before her disappearance, did she behave suspiciously?"

"No," said Frank.

"Did she buy a ticket to anywhere?"

"If she did, she didn't tell me."

"Did she take her passport?"

"The police think so. They couldn't find it in the flat. But Mum can never find it either, so that doesn't mean anything."

"Did she mention travel or journeys or anything like that?"

"No."

"If someone forced her to disappear, then who are the suspects?"

"I don't know," said Frank.

"Why would anyone want her to disappear?"

"I have no idea."

"Does she have any enemies?"

"Not as far I know."

"Did she get threatening phone calls? Or emails? Or letters?"

"She might have, but I never saw them."

"Did anyone want to hurt her?"

"No."

Ben sighed. His list wasn't as useful as he had hoped. He read the next item. "When did she disappear?"

"I don't know," said Frank.

"Where was the last place that she was seen?"

"I don't know that either."

Ben sighed again. He had reached the end of the list without discovering useful information. "Final question," he said. "Who was the last person to see her?"

"I suppose that must have been me," said Frank. "When I went to school."

"Now we're getting somewhere," said Ben. He grabbed his pen, ready to take notes. "Can you remember what she said?"

"'Bye.' Or 'See you later.' Something like that. If she'd said anything unusual, I would have remembered."

"And then what did she do?"

"I don't know. I wasn't there. I left the flat and got the bus to school."

"OK," said Ben. He doodled on the edge of his paper. "If it had been a normal day, just an ordinary Tuesday morning, what would she have done?"

"Gone to work."

"Does she drive? Or get the bus?"

"She goes by bike. Unless it's snowing. Or raining really hard."

"Was it?"

"No."

"So she probably went on her bike?"

"Probably, yes."

"Where's her bike now?"

"I don't know."

"It's not at the flat?"

Frank thought for a second, then shook his head. "No, I don't think so. I can't remember seeing it."

"This is very interesting," said Ben. "We can assume that your mother left the house and went to work on her bicycle. However, she did not return her bicycle to the house. So where is it?"

"At her work?" suggested Kitkat.

"Perhaps," said Ben. "Or perhaps not." He turned to Frank. "On the day in question, your mother left her house on her bicycle – but did she arrive at work?"

"I don't know."

"Finally we're getting somewhere," said Ben. "We have our first line of enquiry." He scribbled on his paper:

1 – Nina left the house on her bike – but did she arrive at work?

Ben looked up. "One more question. Where does she work?"

"Different places on different days," said Frank. "She teaches classes, but she also gives private lessons."

"Where does she teach on Tuesday mornings?"

"The Yoga Studio."

Ben glanced at the display on his phone. "It's twenty to nine. Will they be open now?"

"They should be," said Frank. "They have classes in the evening."

"You've got a phone," said Ben. "Why don't you ring them?"

15

When Frank finished the call, he switched off his phone and told the others what he had discovered.

Last Tuesday, Nina hadn't arrived for work at the Yoga Studio. She was supposed to give a class at ten o'clock. When she missed it, someone rang her mobile and her home number, leaving messages on both, but she never called back. They assumed she must be ill.

She taught private classes on Wednesdays. On Thursday morning, she missed another session at the Yoga Studio. Her colleagues were just discussing what to do when the police arrived. They asked lots of questions, but didn't offer any answers. No one had heard from Nina since and no one had any idea where she might have gone.

"This is great," said Ben. "We're finally getting somewhere. If she didn't get to work, then we know *when* she disappeared. Now we just have to work out *where*. And then we're halfway to finding her. Do you know her route from home to work?"

Frank nodded. "She always goes the same way on her bike."

"Excellent," said Ben. He scribbled on the sheet of paper.

1 – Nina left the flat on her bike – but did she arrive at work?
No.
2 – So where did she go?
3 – Did anyone see her?
4 – Where is her bike?

Harmony peered over his shoulder and read what he had written. "I don't understand why you're writing out all these questions. How are you going to answer them?"

"It's very simple," said Ben. "We know where she started and we know where she was going. We just have to follow her route and we'll find out what happened to her. "

"But she was in Bristol," said Harmony. "How are you going to follow her route?"

"How do you think?"

"I don't know."

"We're going to go to Bristol."

"This is so exciting," said Kitkat, sitting up and clapping her hands. "When are we going?"

"You're not going anywhere," said Ben. "You're much too young."

"But we're the Misfitz! We do everything together!"

"No, we don't."

"Ben's right," said Harmony. "You're too young for this kind of thing. So are we all, actually. I think we should tell Mum and Jeremy what we've discovered."

"Tell them?" gasped Kitkat. "Are you crazy? They'll just tell us we're being silly and we don't know anything."

"I'm going now," said Frank, bored of their arguments and eager to start searching for his mum. "I'm going to get the last train."

"You can't go anywhere," said Harmony. "If you go to Bristol, Mum will kill you. And I don't mean that metaphorically."

"I don't care," said Frank.

"You might when she kills you," said Kitkat.

"She's not my mother," said Frank. "She can't do anything to me."

"You're living in her house," said Harmony.

"With your father. Who is your legal guardian. They can do what they like."

"I don't care," said Frank. "I'm going to Bristol. Right now."

Ben shook his head. "They'll catch us before we even get out of the front door. If we go, we have to go tomorrow. We should sneak out of the house at dawn and catch the train."

"You can't," said Harmony. "When you're not at breakfast, Mum will know where you've gone. She'll come straight after you. If she drives fast enough, she'll get to Bristol before you. When you get off the train, she'll be waiting for you at the station."

"If we can't go now," said Frank, "and we can't go tomorrow, when can we go?"

"We shouldn't go at all," said Harmony. "We should talk to Mum and Jeremy and tell what we've discovered. They'll ring the police, who can deal with this properly."

"I don't trust the police," said Frank. "I trusted them before, but I was wrong. I messed up. I wasted time too. I should have started searching last week. The trail might be cold now. We've got to get to Bristol as soon as possible."

Kitkat had been quiet for some time, but she suddenly perked up. "I know what you should do."

"Yeah?" said Ben. "What should we do?"

"I'll tell you," said Kitkat. "On one condition. You have to let me come too."

"You can't," said Ben.

"Why not?"

"Because you're only seven."

"You're only twelve."

"There's a big difference between seven and twelve."

"Fine," said Kitkat. She folded her arms over her chest and pouted at her brother. "Then I won't tell you my plan."

"We don't care," said Ben. "I bet it's a terrible plan anyway."

"It isn't. It's a really good plan."

Ben sighed. "You know, for five years of my life, I didn't have a little sister. Those were five good years. Then you came along. And everything went wrong."

"You smell," said Kitkat.

"Now you're just being childish."

"That's because I'm only seven. Like you just said. Remember?"

"Stop it, both of you," said Frank. "You're behaving like babies. Kitkat, tell us your plan. If it's bad, we won't do it. If it's good, you deserve to come with us. Even if you're only seven."

Kitkat lowered her voice as if she was going to reveal a great secret. "You should go later."

"That's brilliant," said Ben. "Why didn't I think of that myself?"

"Let her finish," said Frank. He turned to Kitkat. "What do you mean? How much later?"

Kitkat ignored Ben and addressed herself entirely to Frank as if he was the only other person in the room. "Tomorrow morning, we should get dressed and have breakfast and leave the house just like any other day. As if we're going to school. Everything should look completely normal. We should say goodbye to Mum. And walk to the bus stop. Just like normal. But we don't get the bus to school. We get the bus to the train station. And on the bus, you ring my school and your school. You pretend to be our dad. You say we're sick. All four of us. We've all got the same thing. You could say we've got flu. Or you could say we had prawns for supper and they gave us food poisoning. Then we get the train and we go to Bristol."

Frank had started smiling halfway through Kitkat's description of her plan. By the time she finished, he was chuckling out loud. He turned to the others. "You know what? Our little sister is a genius."

16

They left the house after breakfast. Jennifer stood on the front step, waving them off, then turned round and hurried back inside. She had a busy day herself and she wanted to work on her book before going out. She closed the front door and jogged upstairs to her desk.

Ben, Frank, Harmony and Kitkat walked to the bus stop.

Their bus was unusually prompt, arriving only two minutes after them, but they didn't get aboard. Ben could see a couple of kids from King Henry's standing in the middle of the bus. He hoped they hadn't noticed him. The doors slid shut and the bus drove away.

Two more buses came and went. Then the 206 arrived. They boarded and showed their passes to the driver. There were some empty seats at the back. Harmony and Kitkat sat in one row, Frank and Ben in another.

Frank had two numbers written on a scrap of paper. He dialled the first and put the phone to his ear. He spoke in a deep voice. "Hello? Could I speak to Mrs Daniels, please?"

"I'll just fetch her," said the school secretary. "Who is this?"

"Jeremy Fitzroy," said Frank.

The secretary went to find Mrs Daniels, the headmistress of Kitkat's school. She had been Harmony and Ben's headmistress too, and would have recognized their voices, which was why Frank made the call.

Frank held the phone to his ear and stared out of the window, not wanting to meet the others' eyes. He didn't want them to see that he was feeling nervous. He was scared of being caught, but he was even more scared of messing things up.

A woman's voice came on the line. "Hello?"

Frank said, "Good morning, Mrs Daniels. This is Jeremy Fitzroy. Katherine's father."

Frank didn't really sound like his dad. If you knew both of them well, you would never have confused one for the other. But Mrs Daniels had only met Jeremy at a few crowded, noisy parent-teacher evenings and didn't notice anything unusual. She said, "How can I help you, Mr Fitzroy?"

"Katherine can't come to school today," said Frank. "She's not well, I'm afraid."

"Oh, dear. What's wrong?"

"We're not sure. Probably just a cold. We've put her to bed with a hot-water bottle. She'll be back at school tomorrow."

"I hope she has a nice, quiet day," said Mrs Daniels. "Will you wish her all the best from all of us?"

"Of course I will," said Frank. "Thank you very much. Goodbye."

He switched off the phone and glanced down the bus, checking that no one had been listening. Most of the other passengers couldn't have heard anything through their headphones. The others were absorbed in books and newspapers. None of them were interested in four kids or their phone calls.

Frank looked at Ben, Harmony and Kitkat. "That was more difficult than I thought it would be. I don't know if I can do it again."

"Of course you can," said Harmony. "You were brilliant. You sounded just like your dad."

"I didn't," said Frank. But he looked pleased by the compliment. He took a deep breath, then dialled the second number on his list.

This one would be more difficult. He met the head yesterday.

Once again, the phone was answered by a secretary. She asked Frank to wait. A minute passed. Then another. Frank was beginning to give up hope when a voice said, "Hello?"

"Good morning," said Frank. "This is Jeremy Fitzroy."

"Hello, Jeremy. It's David. How can I help?"

"I've got some bad news," said Frank. He had rehearsed exactly what he was going to say, repeating the words over and over to himself, worried that he would forget them. "The three children are sick today. They're all in bed. They can't come to school."

"You sound a bit odd yourself," said the head. "Have you caught the same bug?"

"Yes, I have. We've all got it. But the kids should be back at school tomorrow."

"Thanks for letting me know," said the head. "I'll tell their teachers. Since we're talking anyway, Jeremy, there is one other thing that I'd like to mention. I was planning to call you this week and have a chat. I wanted to talk about Frank."

"Oh. Erm. What did you want to say?"

"I've talked to his teachers and some of them

have found him. . . . How can I put this? He's not the easiest of children."

"Frank will be fine," said Frank. "He's a lot cleverer than he looks."

"Oh, he's certainly clever. We're not worried about that."

"What are you worried about?"

"He doesn't seem happy at all. He hardly speaks to anyone, teachers or pupils. I know he's going through some difficult experiences, but if you could only encourage him to—"

"It's not his fault," interrupted Frank. "It's the other kids. Why don't *they* talk to *him*?"

"I'm sure you're right and this is a two-way process, but it would help if Frank made a little more effort."

"He's trying hard," said Frank. "He's doing his best. But he can't do everything. He's not a superman, OK? He's lost his mum. He's living in a strange house. Couldn't you be a bit more sympathetic?"

"Well, yes," said the head, sounding a little taken aback by this sudden outburst. "I suppose I should."

"Good. Now, if you don't mind, I've got to go and look after the children."

They said goodbye to one another, then Frank switched off the phone and fell back in his seat. His hands were shaking and a line of sweat had collected on his forehead.

The others crowded round, congratulating him.

"You were brilliant," said Kitkat.

"That was fantastic!" said Ben.

"You should be an actor," said Harmony. "I started believing you really were your dad."

Frank wiped the sweat from his forehead and let out a long, exhausted sigh. Then he giggled. The others joined in. Soon all four of them were hunched over, red-faced, snorting with laughter.

Down the bus, other passengers turned to look at them, wondering what was so funny, but the Misfitz didn't care. They just laughed and laughed and laughed till tears ran down their faces.

17

When they emerged from the tube at Paddington Station, Ben, Frank and Harmony checked their phones. No one had rung them. No one had left any messages. They hadn't been caught. Not yet, anyway.

Last night, they had collected all their money. Kitkat emptied her piggy bank. Ben dragged the shoebox from under his bed and tipped out his coins. Harmony took the last of her savings from her purse. They put every penny in a plastic bag.

Ben bought four day returns from a machine. He passed them round. "Keep it safe. We don't have enough to pay for another. If you lose this, you're walking home."

Kitkat said, "How long would that take?"

"It's a hundred miles," said Ben. "You could probably walk about five miles a day. So that's. . ."

"Three weeks," said Frank.

"I can't walk for three weeks!" cried Kitkat.

"Then don't lose your ticket," said Ben.

Kitkat tucked it carefully into the top pocket of her jeans.

Frank searched the electronic boards. The 9.30 to Bristol Temple Meads would be leaving from Platform 5.

They hurried through the ticket barriers and down Platform 5. The train was waiting. At the far end, near the engine, they found four seats around a table.

Ben and Kitkat sat on one side, Harmony and Frank on the other. They stared out of the window at the platform and waited impatiently for the train to leave.

Ben kept expecting to see his mum striding along the platform, searching for her children.

He knew it wasn't going to happen. Jennifer was miles away. As far as she knew, they were at school. And if, by some amazing chance, she discovered that they weren't, it wouldn't even cross her mind that they were sitting at the far end of a train on Platform 5 in Paddington Station.

And yet, knowing all this, he couldn't help worrying that he was going to see her on the other side of the window and hear the rat-ta-ta-tat of her knuckles on the glass.

When the train pulled out of the station, he flopped back in his seat and watched the buildings ease past. At last! They were free!

Later, of course, things would be different. They would have to explain where they had been and why they had lied.

Let's just hope we find Nina, thought Ben. Then none of those questions will matter. We'll be heroes and no one will care we skipped a day at school or told a couple of little white lies.

They left London behind and passed through Reading and Swindon and big empty patches of countryside. They saw two horses galloping through a field and an armada of small boats sailing across a lake and a garden filled with a hundred gnomes.

When they had been travelling for about an hour, Kitkat said, "I'm hungry."

"Me too," said Frank.

"I want some crisps."

"Good plan. Let's go to the buffet."

"We can't afford it," said Ben. "Most of our money went on the tickets and we've got to save the rest for emergencies."

"We don't need the buffet," said Harmony. "I brought elevenses."

She opened her rucksack and tipped its contents on to the table. Before leaving home, she had raided the fridge, the fruit bowl and the cupboards, stealing eight tangerines, a bag of cashew nuts, a big bar of milk chocolate and a whole packet of Jaffa Cakes. She'd also made four sandwiches, two cheese and tomato and two ham and lettuce. There was even a choice of drinks: four little cartons of orange juice and a bottle of fizzy lemonade.

"What about crisps?" said Kitkat. "I wanted crisps."

"Have this instead." Harmony passed her a cheese sandwich. "It's much healthier."

"I don't want healthy. I want crisps."

"Crisps make you fat," said Ben.

"I don't care."

"They'll give you a heart attack," added Harmony.

"I don't care. I want some."

"Then go and buy some," said Ben.

"I don't have any money."

"Then shut up and eat your sandwich."

Kitkat sighed. Last night, they had called her a genius. Now they were telling her to shut up. Things were back to normal.

18

They left the train at Bristol Temple Meads.

Ben glanced at a big round clock hanging on the wall. It was 11.15. Back in London, his classmates would be in French, learning irregular verbs. Lucky them.

They passed through the ticket barriers and the ticket hall, then emerged from the station beside the taxi rank. Drivers were lingering alongside their cars, waiting for fares. They didn't give the Misfitz a second glance, knowing already that four kids wouldn't need a cab.

"This way," said Frank.

A light drizzle was falling. People huddled under umbrellas.

They joined a silent queue at the bus stands outside the station.

The bus came soon. They stepped aboard. Ben handed the bag of coins to Frank, who paid their fares.

They found some seats at the back. The doors closed and the bus lurched forward.

Ben stared out of the rain-speckled window, watching Bristol, trying to spot the differences between this city and his home, but both of them looked oddly similar. The houses, people and cars could have been transported from one city to the other and no one would have noticed the difference.

They had been travelling for fifteen minutes when Frank said, "It's the next stop." He pressed the bell to alert the driver.

Ben, Kitkat and Harmony followed Frank off the bus and found themselves in a busy main road packed with shops and shoppers.

"This way," said Frank and marched down the street. The others jogged after him. If they had hesitated for a moment, they would have got lost in a strange street in a strange city with no idea where to go.

Frank darted down a side street. The noise and bustle fell away quickly. Soon, the only sounds were birdsong, their four pairs of footsteps and a radio playing in one of the houses. The rain had stopped. They passed a restaurant. Inside, upturned chairs were perched on the tables. They turned the corner and walked up a narrow street lined by tall, thin houses.

A man was washing his car, soaping water over the windscreen with a red cloth. He nodded to Frank, who nodded back.

A woman was standing by a ground-floor window, her hands pressed against the glass. She was wearing a blue dressing gown and a red woollen hat. When she saw the Misfitz, she pointed at them with both hands and yelled. Her words were muffled by the glass.

"Who's she?" asked Ben.

"Our crazy neighbour," said Frank.

"Why's she crazy?" said Kitkat.

"I don't know," said Frank. "Maybe she had an unhappy childhood."

Kitkat shook her head. "I don't mean what made her crazy. I mean how do you know she's crazy. What does she do?"

"Shouts at people. Walks round naked. Normal crazy stuff."

On the other side of the crazy woman's house, Frank stopped at a three-storey building with a bright red front door.

"This is it," he said, pulling a bunch of keys from his pocket. "Welcome to Château Fitzroy."

He unlocked the door and led them into a dark hallway. A sleek new racing bike was propped against the wall.

Ben said, "Is that your mum's?"

"No, that belongs to the German guy who lives on the ground floor. Hers isn't nearly so nice."

Three wooden shelves fastened to the wall held post for the three flats. The lower two were empty, but the upper one overflowed with envelopes. Frank scooped up the lot and sorted through them, discarding leaflets for pizza delivery and cards for cab companies, checking the labels on the others.

"No more mysterious postcards," he said. "Just a bunch of bills."

He tucked the post under his arm and led the way up the stairs.

19

Frank swung open the front door. He paused for a second, listening, hoping to hear footsteps or his mother's voice, then tossed the post on to a low table and hurried through the flat, checking every room.

The house had been divided into three flats, one on each floor. Frank and Nina lived at the top. They had the furthest to climb, but they got the best views.

Compared to 32 Cardinal Road, the flat was small, cramped, cluttered and amazingly untidy. There were plants everywhere. The walls were covered in postcards, paintings and rugs. Any spare space was filled with some odd bit of junk: a broken vase, a wine bottle with a candle stuck in the stem, a map of Nepal, an old teddy bear without any eyes, a grandfather clock, a rolled-up yoga mat. Ben could understand why the police couldn't find Nina's passport or driver's licence, and why she was never able to find them herself.

Frank's own room was about half the size of Ben's and cluttered with books, comics, clothes and enough computer equipment to run a small country. It was obvious that Frank didn't have the type of mother who stood in the doorway and yelled, "This place is a tip! You're not having any supper till you've put everything where it belongs."

There was a dead wasp on the kitchen table and a big black spider in the bath, but that was all. According to Frank, he couldn't even see any evidence of a police search. The flat looked as if nothing had been touched.

Ben saw a handwritten note on the kitchen table.

Mum
I've gone to London with Dad.
I want to stay here and wait for you but he
won't let me.
If you come home, please ring me.
Frank

"When did you write this?"

"Last thing before I left," said Frank. He

crumpled the note into a ball and tossed it in the bin.

Ben glanced at the display on his phone. "It's nearly twelve. I'd better get going. Will you print out the stuff?"

"Sure."

Frank took his laptop to his bedroom and plugged it into the printer. He printed out a colour picture and offered it to Ben.

The photograph had been taken at a picnic on a clear bright day. Nina was holding a plastic plate in one hand and a glass of white wine in the other. She was wearing old jeans and a long white shirt, and grinning at the camera.

Ben said, "Does she still look like this?"

"When she's in a good mood."

A second sheet eased out of the printer, a map of Bristol. Frank had drawn a red line on the map, showing Nina's route to work.

"We're here," said Frank, pointing to one end of the red line. "She always cycles along the same roads." He ran his finger along the line, mimicking his mum's journey. "It takes her twenty minutes. You should be able to walk it in two hours."

They had agreed to divide into three separate units: Ben would follow Nina's route to work,

Frank would investigate Nina's computer and Harmony and Kitkat would search the flat.

Ben folded the map and the photo in half, and tucked them in his pocket. He waved to the girls, who had already started searching the sitting room, hunting through the bookshelves, sorting through piles of paper. "Good luck with your stuff."

"Thanks," said Kitkat. "Good luck with yours."

Harmony said, "Do you need anything else?"

"No."

"If you get lost," said Frank, "call me."

"I will."

"And if you find anything."

"As soon as."

"See you later."

Ben let himself out of the front door and jogged down the stairs.

He glanced at his phone. It was 11.56. He had to move fast. If the plan worked, he had three or four hours before they had to catch their train back to London.

If the plan worked.

I've got three hours, thought Ben. Four at the most. To find a missing woman.

I'd better get going.

20

When Ben left the house, the first thing he saw was the crazy neighbour on the other side of the street. She was still standing in her front room, her hands pressed against the glass. When she noticed Ben, she shouted at him. Remembering what Frank had said, he hurried past, pretending he hadn't seen her.

Ben stopped beside the man who was washing his car and said, "Excuse me? Do you know Nina Fitzroy?"

"Of course I know Nina. You're a friend of Frank's, are you?"

"I'm his stepbrother. He's staying with me in London."

"Is there any news of her? We heard she's missing."

"That's what I wanted to ask," said Ben. "Have you seen her since last Tuesday morning?"

"No, I haven't. Nor has anyone in the street. The

police have been asking questions at every house. If any of us knew anything, we'd have told them."

Ben thanked him and continued along the street. He turned left, then right, following the red line that Frank had drawn on the map.

As he walked, he looked at the photo again, studying Nina's features. She looked younger than he had remembered, and happier too. He realized he probably wouldn't have recognized her if he'd passed her in the street – and he certainly wouldn't have been able to describe what she looked like. He was glad he had the photo. He was going to need it.

When he came to the main road, he went into the newsagent on the corner and showed the photo to the woman behind the counter. "Excuse me? I'm looking for this woman. Do you know her?"

"Everyone knows Nina," said the newsagent. "How's Frank?"

"He's fine."

"Where's he staying?"

"With me. In London. I'm his brother."

"Ah, his brother. She's told me all about you. And your sisters. And your dad. He sounds like a difficult man, your father."

"He's not actually my father," said Ben. "He's my stepfather. My real father lives in California."

"What does he do there?"

"He works in the film business," said Ben. He had the sense that he was wasting valuable time, chatting about his family, when he should be searching for Nina. He brandished the photo. "You don't know where she might be?"

"I have no idea. That's what I told the police. They've been here twice in the past week."

Before Ben could ask any more questions, the newsagent excused herself and served a customer who wanted to buy a newspaper and a lottery ticket. When the customer had gone, Ben asked when the newsagent had last seen Nina. "Did you see her on Tuesday morning? Did she come in here? Or go past on her bike?"

"The police asked me that too, but I just can't remember. I'm so sorry."

Ben thanked her for her help and continued down the street. He stopped in every shop and asked the same questions.

Near the flat, several shopkeepers knew Nina's name and almost all recognized her face. Many had already been interviewed by the police. The butcher was sure that he had seen her cycling past on Tuesday morning. The greengrocer gave Ben a free apple and wished him luck. The woman in the delicatessen had a parcel for Nina, a special cheese that she'd ordered ten days ago. "I'm keeping it for her," she said. "Send my love to Frank. Tell him we're thinking about him."

Further down the street, a homeless man was squatting in the doorway of a disused shop. He recognized Nina's photo and said she often stopped for a chat, but he couldn't remember seeing her for at least a week.

Ben went into a dingy off-licence called Bargain Booze. The walls were stacked with bottles and plastered with big orange notices promising that OUR PRICES WON'T BE BEATEN and CHEAPEST BEER IN BRISTOL! A grey-haired man was leaning on the counter, poring over a crumpled newspaper, reading the racing pages. He had bloodshot eyes and his breath smelt like an unwashed wine glass. "Oh, yes," he said, jabbing the photo with his forefinger. "I know her."

"Are you sure?" said Ben.

"No doubt about it. I know all my customers. She smokes roll-ups and drinks Chardonnay. Unless she's come into some money and then she'll treat herself to a bottle of champagne. What more do you want to know?"

"She's gone missing," said Ben. "She hasn't been

seen since last Tuesday. Do you know what's happened to her?"

"Tuesday..." The grey-haired man closed his eyes for a moment, trying to remember. He opened his eyes again and shook his head. "I don't think I've seen her for a couple of weeks. Sorry."

It was slow work. After half an hour, Ben was still within sight of the newsagent where he had started, but he hadn't discovered any useful information.

He decided to speed up.

The police had been here already. They had computers, cars and enough people to question everyone in the city. If they hadn't found her, how would he?

He started skipping shops, walking quickly along his route and only stopping to ask questions in significant places. Shops on corners or at junctions. Anywhere that Nina might have deviated from her usual route.

As he got further from the flat, fewer people recognized Nina. Shopkeepers squinted at the picture, then shook their heads. "Sorry, son. Never seen her before."

The police didn't appear to have bothered coming this far. They had simply talked to the shopkeepers who worked near the house. They obviously thought there was no point searching any further.

Maybe they were right.

Ben wondered if he was wasting his time. The road was full of traffic. Thousands of people went past these shops every hour. Thousands of vehicles too. Why would anyone remember one woman who might or might not have cycled past a week ago?

He was tired and hungry. His feet ached. His belly was complaining. It was lunch time, but all he had eaten was elevenses on the train and an apple from the greengrocer, and he wasn't likely to get anything else.

He trudged down the street, following Nina's route, asking the same questions again and again, and hearing the same answers.

No one had seen her. No one recognized her face. No one knew her. No one could help him.

Just as he was beginning to despair, he had a breakthrough.

21

There were six separate spaces in the flat: the hallway, the kitchen, the bathroom, the sitting room and two bedrooms.

They started with the sitting room, working their way methodically from one wall to the other, running their fingers along the edge of the carpet, shaking out rugs, turning over cushions, opening books, picking up pots, delving down the back of the sofa. Their main quarry was Nina's passport – if they found it, they could be sure she hadn't gone to India – but Frank hoped that they might uncover some other interesting evidence too. A letter, perhaps. A receipt or a ticket. Anything, in fact, which offered some clue about her plans.

Frank searched his own room, just in case Nina had hidden her passport there, then came into the sitting room and worked alongside his sisters.

Kitkat said, "What are you doing here? Aren't you meant to be looking at your mum's computer?"

"I will in a minute," said Frank. "I'll help you first. We'll work faster with three people."

Even so, they made slow progress. Searching the sitting room took twenty minutes. They found an old remote control, an unopened packet of sunflower seeds and £2.52 in coins, but no passport, driver's licence, ticket, receipt or relevant evidence of any sort.

Nina's bedroom took another half an hour, but proved no more informative. By the time that they reached the kitchen, they were beginning to get tired and irritable.

"This is hard work," said Kitkat. "I need a rest. Shall we have lunch?"

"We don't have time," said Frank. "We're in a hurry."

"I've got low blood sugar. I might faint."

"You're not going to faint," said Frank.

"I might. I've done it before. I hit my head on the edge of the table and I had to have three stitches."

"How about a glass of water?" said Harmony.

"That's boring."

"You could have a cup of tea," suggested Frank. "Or some juice?"

"Juice would be OK."

"I'd like tea," said Harmony.

"Tea is there." Frank pointed to a cupboard. "I'll put the kettle on. And there are some cartons of juice in the cupboard in the hall."

Kitkat fetched a carton of mango juice and poured a couple of glasses. She handed one to Frank and kept the other. Harmony made a cup of peppermint tea for herself.

"Do you have any crisps?" said Kitkat.

"Mum doesn't approve of crisps. You can have some seaweed or a rice cake."

"No, thanks."

"There might be some biscuits."

"What sort?"

"You can look for yourself. They're in that cupboard."

Kitkat stood on a chair, opened the cupboard and looked inside. She could see about fifty boxes and cartons of all shapes and sizes. Most of them looked as if they hadn't been touched this century. She opened the nearest and found some old spices, cardamom pods and coriander seeds, which released a wonderful smell when she took the top off the tin.

"Hmmm. Delicious. How about going out for curry?"

"I told you already," said Frank. "We don't have time to eat. Come on, stop mucking about. Let's get back to work."

Kitkat took no notice of her brother. She wanted a biscuit and she wasn't going to stop till she found one. She opened another tin and found a packet of rubbery dried apricots. She opened a third and found some black tea leaves. She was determined to find a biscuit, so she kept going, opening more jars and more boxes and more cartons and more tins, till she finally found something that she actually wanted.

She stepped down from the chair and offered the battered old tin to Frank. "Hey, big bro, have a biscuit."

"I don't want one."

"Go on."

"No, thanks. I've got work to do. I don't have time for biscuits."

"You'll like it, I promise."

"I just told you, I don't want one."

"Have one anyway. It'll be good for you."

"Fine," said Frank. "If I must."

He put his hand inside the tin and pulled out his mother's passport.

22

Boxes of tattered old books were stacked outside the window. A handwritten sign announced ALL BOOKS £1. Through the window, Ben could see a dark shop packed with bookshelves and a single customer, reading in a corner. He pushed the door. A bell jangled. The customer glanced up, then returned to his book. Behind a wooden desk on the other side of the shop, a bald man was hunched over an old black book. He looked up and said, "Good afternoon. Can I help?"

Ben showed him the photo and started explaining what he was looking for. Before he had said more than a few words, the bald bookseller interrupted him.

"Oh, I know Nina." The bookseller closed his book. A cloud of dust rose from the pages. "I know her son too. They're often here. Are you a friend of his?"

"We're brothers," said Ben.

"I didn't know Nina had two children."

"She doesn't. We're stepbrothers. His dad is married to my mum."

"Aha. And you're helping him search for her?"

"Yes."

"I wish I could help. She's a lovely woman. And one of my few regular customers. She comes in here once or twice a month and always buys a book."

"Did you see her last Tuesday morning?"

"Tuesday. . . Was that the day she disappeared?"

"Yes."

"I'm sorry, I can't remember. I've seen her recently, I'm sure of that, but I don't know when."

Ben's shoulders slumped.

"Wait a minute," said the bald man. "Tuesday. . . Let me see." He reached for a small black diary and skimmed through the pages. "That's right. I wasn't here on Tuesday. I went to an auction in Cardiff. Let me call my daughter." He opened a door at the back of the shop and shouted, "Sophie! Sophie! Can you come here for a second?"

Sophie turned out to be a slim woman in her twenties who ran a book-binding business in the back of the shop. On Tuesday, she had been arranging the boxes of cheap books on the pavement when Nina cycled past.

"She shouted something," said Sophie. "I can't remember what. But she was happy, I remember that. She was grinning."

Ben said, "You're sure it was Tuesday?"

"It was definitely Tuesday. That's been my only day in the shop for the past month."

Ben thanked Sophie and her father. He wrote down his name and phone number in case they remembered anything else. Then he left the bookshop and stood in the street, staring at the map, working out where he was.

He had walked about a quarter of Nina's route and he was still on the right track. Last Tuesday, she had come past the bookshop on her way to work. Somewhere between here and the Yoga Studio, she had disappeared. But where? And why? And how?

He glanced at the display on his phone.

It was almost half past one.

Better hurry.

Ben walked along the road. He passed a disused chapel. The stone steps were littered with old bottles and cigarette butts. Any spare brickwork had been covered with graffiti. High on the wall,

Ben could see a large white poster printed with black letters:

The Alpha Course
An Opportunity to Discover the Meaning of Life
Starting here on Wednesday 8th Oc

The rest of the poster was hidden under other, newer posters, advertising clubs and gigs and songs by bands he'd never heard of.

He came to a garage selling second-hand cars. The salesman waved Ben away without even listening to his questions.

He walked down the hill and under a railway bridge.

That was when he had his second breakthrough.

23

Frank placed his mother's battered old computer on the kitchen table. It was actually one of his old ones. He'd donated it to his mother and set it up for her, making everything as straightforward as possible. She still asked him for help all the time.

He didn't open it immediately.

He didn't want to.

The computer glared at him, taunting him, tempting him to lift its lid and expose his mother's secrets.

He had never gone through her files. He could have done. He was often alone in the flat. And he knew his mother's passwords. She wrote them on a postcard and kept it in her desk. But he respected her privacy. He didn't want to discover her secrets, just as he didn't want her to know his.

He knew he had to go through her computer now. He didn't have any other option. He was determined to follow every avenue that might lead to her.

What if he learnt something about his mother that he didn't want to know?

He reminded himself of one important fact: he would do anything to help her.

Anything.

Even if he had to hurt himself.

Or her.

He still didn't want to open her computer.

He couldn't distract himself by talking to Harmony and Kitkat. He had sent them outside to interview the neighbours. They now knew that Nina definitely hadn't gone to India. She couldn't have left the country without her passport. But if she had gone somewhere else – if she had walked out of the house on Tuesday with a bag, for instance, or climbed into a friend's car – then someone might have seen her.

He reached into a kitchen cupboard and lifted out a large glass jug. He filled it at the cold tap and walked from room to room, watering the plants. Several looked bedraggled. One was surrounded by dead petals. The leaves of another had turned brown. Two appeared to have died, but he fed them anyway, hoping they'd come back to life.

He returned the jug to its place in the cupboard, then sat in his mother's favourite chair and opened her laptop on his knees.

He left her email to last. First, he went through her accounts.

Her deposit account contained £3,821.56 and hadn't been touched for almost a month.

She had £240.22 in her current account. A direct debit had withdrawn £46 on Tuesday, the day that she disappeared, but that had been an automated payment and would have gone through without the need for any human interference.

Her credit card had last been used on Sunday afternoon. Frank remembered when. They had gone to an exhibition at the Arnolfini and eaten lunch in the café afterwards. A friend of his mum's had met them there, an artist called Dominic, who talked about himself a lot. Nina laughed loudly at his jokes, the way she did when she liked someone. Frank read a book and tried to ignore them.

He checked her phone bill. The last call had been made on Monday evening. He didn't recognize the number. He rang it, dialling 141 first to hide his own number. A man's voice said, "Hello?"

Frank said, "Who is this?"

"Dominic Preston," said the voice. "Who's this?"

Frank switched off the phone.

Over the years, several different men had passed through his mother's life. Some were friends. Others were lovers. A few had been something in-between. Frank liked two or three of them, and hated two or three, and hadn't cared very much about any of the others.

When Nina's boyfriends met Frank for the first time, they always acted as if they were his new best friend, cracking jokes and trying to make him laugh. When that didn't work, they usually tried to talk to him about football.

As soon as they learnt that he played chess, they usually challenged him to a game, but none of them wanted to play more than once. They didn't like being beaten so quickly.

He wondered whether the police had investigated Nina's latest bloke. And, if so, what they had found.

He returned to his mother's computer and googled "Dominic Preston". It was a common name, but not too common. There were only a couple of thousand hits. A Scottish singer, a Texan doctor, a footballer in Arizona, an estate agent in New York, a banker in London and a painter in Bristol. With his own website.

Frank flicked through every page on Dominic Preston's site, checking out his paintings, a list of his exhibitions and a black-and-white photo of the artist. Frank recognized the man who had joined them for Sunday lunch. He stared into the eyes of Dominic Preston and wondered whether he held the clue to Nina's disappearance.

Frank turned to his own computer and started a new file called DOMINIC PRESTON, adding all the information that he knew about the man: his name, his accent, his physical description, his job, his phone number, his website and his email address.

He went back to his mother's computer and started reading through her emails. None had been read since Tuesday morning, but lots had arrived. Several had been sent from the Yoga Studio and many more were from her students, asking where she was and why she hadn't been in touch.

He looked at the recent emails that his mother had written. The last had been sent early on Tuesday morning. She must have written it just before she left the house and went to work. Frank couldn't imagine it had anything to do with her disappearance: Nina had simply replied to one of her students, promising to bring a book about Indian religion to the next yoga class.

Frank worked backwards, reading through the emails that Nina had written and received. He found messages from her students, her friends, his father, Nina's mother, her aunt, a cousin in Australia and all kinds of people with names that meant nothing to him.

He tried to skip references to himself, but he couldn't help reading a few. One of his teachers had complained about his behaviour. His gran asked what he wanted for his birthday. One of Nina's ex-boyfriends blamed Frank for breaking up their relationship.

He skimmed through endless messages about yoga. He found a long correspondence with Dominic Preston and was horrified to discover that his mother had met him on a dating site. He wanted to shake her. Didn't she know the internet was dangerous?

He forwarded every one of Dominic Preston's emails to himself. When he got back to London, he would send extracts directly to the police.

He didn't find anything which explained how or why his mother had disappeared, but he gradually built up a portrait of her life, and he was surprised to realize the limitations of his own knowledge. Other people knew different parts of her. With him, she was always a mother and sometimes a friend. With them, she was a daughter, a cousin, a colleague, a teacher, a friend or a lover. She had opinions that he wouldn't have recognized as hers. She mentioned events in her own life that he knew nothing about. She was a different person to each of them. And who could say which was the real Nina Fitzroy?

24

On the other side of the railway bridge, Ben emerged at a crossroads. There was a café on one corner and an antiques shop on another. Several nearby houses were covered in scaffolding.

Three teenagers were walking along the road, two boys and a girl, wearing jeans and hoodies. They looked Ben up and down as if they were deciding what to do with him. To his relief, they walked straight past and carried on up the hill.

At the crossroads, Ben glanced at his map. Which direction should he take?

A train rumbled over the bridge. The noise was loud enough to shake his bones.

He looked at the café. Through its big windows, he could see three people: two diners at a table and a waitress in a black uniform. The waitress had to be able to see everything that happened in the street. If she had been there last Tuesday morning, she would have seen Nina on her bicycle. He hurried across the road and went into the café.

As soon as he opened the door, he was greeted by the strong smell of frying bacon. Two builders were eating at one table. The waitress was clearing another. She turned round, balancing three plates in her small hands, and smiled at Ben. "Can I help you?"

"I'm looking for someone," said Ben. He thrust the photo at her. "Have you ever seen this woman before?"

The waitress peered at the photo, then at Ben. "She's pretty. Who is she?"

"My stepbrother's mother."

"Your stepbrother's mother." The waitress thought for a moment, then nodded. "OK, I understand. And why are you looking for her?"

"She cycles past here on her way to work," said Ben. "Last Tuesday, she left home, but she never arrived at her job. She's disappeared. The police can't find her. So we're going to."

"Who's we?"

"My stepbrother and my sisters and me."

"That's a lovely story." The waitress looked at the photo again, staring longer and harder, searching her memory, then shook her head. "I'm sorry, sweetheart. I wish I could help, but I've never seen her before."

Ben thanked her and turned to go. As he was walking towards the door, a voice called him in a strong foreign accent. "Hey! Boy! Yes, you!"

One of the builders was beckoning to him from the other side of the café. They had been listening to his conversation with the waitress.

"Let's see. Come here and show us the picture."

Ben walked over to them and placed the photo on the table.

Both builders were wearing paint-splattered T-shirts and yellow fluorescent jerkins. Their faces were dirty. Their hands too. But they had kindly faces and Ben immediately trusted them.

"I told you so," said one of the builders to the other. He pointed at the photo. "She *is* the one."

The second builder shook his head and replied to him in a foreign language. They spoke quickly to one another. Ben wished he could understand what they were saying.

They soon seemed to reach some kind of agreement, because they turned to Ben and one of them said, "This woman – you lose her on Tuesday? Yes?"

"Yes," said Ben. "She left home in the morning.

But she never got to work. She went missing."

"We have seen her."

"We have *maybe* seen her," said the second builder. "We are not knowing if this is the same woman."

"This is definitely the same woman," said the first builder. "There is not question."

Ben said, "Where did you see her?"

"Sit down," said one of the builders, shifting chairs to make space for Ben at the table. "You want tea?" Without waiting for an answer, he waved to the waitress. "One more tea, please. For the boy." He turned to Ben. "You hungry? You want lunch? A bacon sandwich? Some eggs, maybe?"

"I'm fine, thanks," said Ben. He was starving, but he couldn't waste time now. He was impatient to discover more about Nina. "Where did you see her? Here? In this café?"

The two builders answered quickly, each of them speaking over the other, as if they were rushing to get their answers out as fast as possible.

"Yes, here."

"Near here."

"She is crashing her bicycle."

"We can show you."

"Is no good bicycle."

"Not for riding."

"Only for scrapping."

"Not even that."

"Is totally wrecked."

"Wait, wait," said Ben. "Can't you just tell me what you saw?"

The two builders laughed. They introduced themselves, offering their big, dusty hands for Ben to shake. "I am Pavel," said the younger of them. "And this is Konrad."

"I am very pleased to meet you," said Konrad, shaking Ben's hand. "What is your name?"

Ben told them his name and shook hands with them both.

Pavel had a skinny face, short blond hair and an easy, confident smile. One of his front teeth was missing. He had a red dragon tattooed on the back of his hand, its snout nestling by his thumb and its scaly tail curling up his sleeve.

Konrad was older and his black hair was thinning on the top of his head. Deep frown lines surrounded his eyes and mouth. Around his neck, he was wearing a little wooden cross on a silver chain.

Konrad explained that he and Pavel were working on a house across the street. They had been there for the last three weeks, fitting a new kitchen and bathroom. The owner was paying them a good wage to finish as quickly as possible, so they were working seven days a week, ten hours a day. Last Tuesday morning, they had heard a crash.

"We are in kitchen downstairs. We hear noise. One big crash. Very loud. We know at once, someone is hurt."

"We stop everything, drop everything," said Pavel. "Run out of house."

"We find one bike, one woman, lying on road."

"The car," said Pavel. "He drive away."

"He is criminal."

"I run after him and look for number, but not quick enough."

"He maybe thinks he killed her. He thinks he go to prison. So he runs away."

"We go to woman. She has blood on face. She is confused. She says nothing. I hold her hand. I talk to her. I say, 'Are you OK? Are you hurt?' Konrad, he rings nine, nine, nine."

"I ask for ambulance," said Konrad. "Come quickly, I say. Come now."

"We talk to the woman, but she don't talk back. I don't know why."

"The ambulance arrive. Then the police."

"The ambulance take her away."

"The police go too."

"And that's the end. We come back to work."

Ben said, "Did the police ask you many questions?"

"They didn't say nothing," said Pavel.

"They take our names and our numbers and say they come and find us," said Konrad. "But they never do."

Ben pushed the photo towards them. "Was it her?"

Konrad shrugged his shoulders. "This is maybe her," he said. "Or maybe not. I don't know for sure."

"I know her anywhere," said Pavel, planting his forefinger on the photo. "This is her."

"Will you show me where it happened?" said Ben.

Pavel and Konrad didn't even hesitate. They hadn't finished their meals, but they pushed back their chairs and led him out of the café.

"Don't take them away," Konrad called to the waitress, gesturing at their plates, which were still piled high with bacon, beans and toast. "We'll be back."

"I know you will," said the waitress. She crossed her arms over her chest and watched them leave.

25

Konrad and Pavel led Ben across the road and down a quiet suburban street called Bradfield Avenue. Ben recognized the name. If he hadn't gone into the café, he would have come down here himself, following Nina's route on her bicycle.

"We hear the crash," said Pavel. "Like one big bang."

"She is lying here. The car is there." Konrad pointed to the end of Bradfield Avenue. "He is running away."

"And the bike?" asked Ben.

"All smashed up."

"It is horrible," said Pavel. "Like a bad dream."

"Come, you can see."

Konrad and Pavel were working in a large, semi-detached house, set back from the main road. A skip sat outside, piled with all kinds of junk –

empty paint pots, old piping, a chair, a window frame, half a bath and broken bits of timber.

There was a black wooden gate at the side of the house. Konrad pulled a bunch of keys from his dungarees, selected one and unlocked the gate.

Left with Pavel, Ben felt awkward. He couldn't think of anything to say. He just smiled, then stared at the ground.

He suddenly remembered what his mum always said about strangers. You can talk to them, she said. You should be polite. You can answer their questions. But you should never, ever go anywhere with them.

Was he being stupid? Should he not have come here with these two strangers? Maybe they were lying to him. Maybe they were going to tempt him into the house and murder him.

He lifted his head and looked around. He was standing in an ordinary street, surrounded by houses. If he shouted for help, people would come running. He told himself to stop being so paranoid. These two strangers weren't going to hurt him – they were going to help him.

"You English?" said Pavel.

"Yes."

"From Bristol?"

"No, I'm from London."

"Oh, London." Pavel nodded wisely. "I have been there one time. You know Victoria Station?"

"I know where it is."

"I have been to Victoria Station," said Pavel. "Also I have been to the Piccadilly Circus and Ravenscourt Park. You know these places?"

"I know Piccadilly Circus," said Ben. "But I've never heard of Ravenscourt Park."

"Really?" Pavel was surprised. "You should go there. Is very nice place. Not far from Hammersmith. You know Hammersmith?"

Before Ben could reply, he saw Konrad emerging from the garden with what had once been a red bicycle. Both pedals had been broken off. The crossbar was bent in half. Shards of red paint had peeled away from the frame, showing the silver metal underneath, and the snapped chain hung hopelessly from the gears.

If the bike looks like that, thought Ben, what happened to Nina?

"We keep," said Konrad. "For when she comes back."

"Don't know why," said Pavel. "She never will want. We should put on skip."

"Better to keep," said Konrad.

"Can I take a picture?" said Ben.

"You do what you want."

Ben pulled out his phone and took three pictures from different angles. He could show them to Frank later and find out if this was definitely his mum's bike. Then he turned to the builders and said, "Do you know what happened to her? Where did she go from here?"

"To hospital," said Konrad. "The ambulance comes here and takes her away."

"Where did they take her? Which hospital?"

"The big one," said Pavel. "Bristol Royal Infirmary."

"How do you know?"

"Because they told us."

"Who?"

"The ambulance men."

"Is not far," said Konrad. "I went to Bristol Royal Infirmary one time. When I fall from scaffolding. They are good doctors. They will look after her good. You don't have to worry."

Ben remembered Jeremy saying that the police had checked every hospital in Bristol, but Nina hadn't been admitted to any of them. That didn't make sense. Had the police missed her? Or failed to ask the right questions? Was she still in the hospital now?

What about the postcard? How could she send a postcard if she was in hospital?

And why would she say she was in India?

There was only one way to find out.

"I'm going to go there," he said. "Which way is it?"

Pavel pointed back towards the café. "You must go that way. Go left. Then right. Walk on till you find big street with many shops. Then ask someone for more directions."

"How long will it take me to get there?"

"Maybe twenty minutes if you walk fast. Maybe one half hour."

"I'd better get going," said Ben. "Thank you very much for your help. I don't know what I'd have done if I hadn't met you."

"No problem," said Pavel.

"You come back," said Konrad. "Tell us if you find your mother. We want to know, yes?"

Ben promised to come back and thanked them again, then turned and hurried down the street. He hadn't taken more than a few paces when a voice shouted after him.

"Hey! Ben!" It was Konrad. He was pointing to a

white van parked in the street. "I take you there. Come on, is much quicker."

Ben knew he shouldn't accept a lift from a stranger, but he was in a hurry. And Konrad had a kind face. He jogged across the road.

26

Ben rang Frank from the van. He said, "I think I've found her."

"You *think*?" snapped Frank. "What's that supposed to mean? Have you or haven't you?"

"I haven't actually seen her yet. But I think I know where she is."

"Where is she?"

Ben explained how he had met Konrad and Pavel, and what they had told him. "Konrad's driving me to the hospital now."

"Which hospital?"

"Bristol Royal Infirmary. Do you know it?"

"I'll meet you outside," said Frank, ignoring the question. "I'm going to leave here right now. I'll bring the others. You'll get there before us, but don't go in. Wait for me at the main entrance."

Ben didn't argue. He could understand why Frank wanted to be the first person to see his mother. If their situations were reversed, he would have felt the same.

When Ben switched off the phone, Konrad said, "Everything is good?"

"Everything's fine," said Ben. "My brother is going to meet me at the hospital."

"Is best for him to see his mother, yes?"

"I think so," said Ben.

Konrad drove fast. He knew exactly where he was going. He told Ben about his accident. Since then, he had returned to the hospital several times for X-rays and check-ups. He touched his side. "Is OK now. But it is hurting when it is raining. Don't know why."

Konrad parked the van in a side street and walked with Ben to the entrance of the Bristol Royal Infirmary. Ben assured him that he didn't mind waiting alone, but Konrad insisted on staying there till Frank arrived.

They were surrounded by people puffing on cigarettes. This was the nearest place to the hospital where you were allowed to smoke, so doctors, nurses and patients hurried out of the doors with a packet of cigarettes in one hand and a box of matches in the other, ready to light up as soon as possible. They huddled in small groups in the fresh air, dragging deep draughts of smoke into their lungs.

Konrad suddenly said, "I have son in my own country. He is your age. Younger, maybe. His name is Teodor. You know this name?"

"There's a boy at my school called Theo," said Ben. "His real name is Theodore. Is that the same?"

"Yes, this is the same. If my son come to England, his name is Theo. But we call him Teodor. I have not seen him for seven months. He lives in my village with my wife. If there is problem with her, I hope people will help him. Like I help you. Do you understand?"

"Of course I do," said Ben. "Everyone has to help one another."

"This is true. But let me tell you something. It does not happen. Not in Poland, not in England. People only care about himself."

"You don't," said Ben. "You're helping me."

"No, you are wrong," said Konrad. "I am also only caring about myself. When I help you, I feel good about my son. This is good for me. Do you understand?"

"I think so," said Ben.

"I miss him very much. But it is best for me to

be here and him to be there. I make more money, he has better life." Konrad sighed. "Poland is a beautiful country. Teodor is happy there, I think. One day, you can come and visit us. With your brother. And your mother."

"I have two brothers," said Ben. "And two sisters."

"Then you must all come to Poland. The whole family. You will have one very good holiday." Konrad smiled, then fell into an abrupt silence, staring at the ground as if he were searching for a lost coin.

27

"There is no one by that name in the hospital," said the blonde woman at the reception desk. She had big pink glasses perched on her nose and a pair of pale blue earrings which matched the colour of her eyes.

"Was she here on Tuesday?" said Ben.

"She's never been here at all. Not now. Not last week. Not ever."

"But she came here," insisted Konrad. "In the ambulance."

"No, she didn't," said the receptionist. "I've checked the entire list of admissions. There isn't anyone called Nina Fitzroy. In fact, last Tuesday, there was no one called Fitzroy at all."

"What if she couldn't give her name?" said Ben. "What if she was unconscious?"

"That would be marked on the computer," said the receptionist. "And it isn't."

"What if she gave the wrong name?" said Frank. "She was hit on the head. Maybe she was confused and gave a different name."

"It's very unlikely," said the receptionist. "If someone is unconscious, we look in their wallet or their purse, and find out who they really are. If they seem confused and there's the slightest chance that they could have given the wrong name, we make rigorous checks to ensure that we've identified them correctly."

"Maybe there was a mistake," said Ben. "Could you check if anyone else arrived here who had been in a car crash? She was knocked off her bike on Bradfield Avenue. She hurt her head. She came here in an ambulance. Could you see if that fits anyone from last Tuesday?"

"We don't make mistakes," said the receptionist.

"Couldn't you just have a look?"

"I'm very busy." The receptionist gestured at the queue which had already built up behind Ben, Frank and Konrad. "If there weren't so many people here, I might be able to help, but I can't do anything now. I'm sorry. Could you step aside, please." She peered round Ben. "Who's next?"

Konrad sighed. Frank turned away. But Ben refused to give up. He leaned forward and said in a quiet voice, "Can't you just have a quick look at the computer? It won't take more than a minute and it might change someone's life." He pointed at Frank. "She's his mother. She's been missing for a week. Can't you imagine how he's feeling?"

"If she's been missing for a week," said the receptionist, "he should talk to the police."

"He has. They can't find her. Which is why we're looking for her ourselves." Ben turned round and spoke loudly enough that everyone in the queue could hear what he was saying. "I'm sure no one will mind waiting for one more minute if it means a boy might find his mother."

Up and down the queue, people shook their heads and said they didn't mind at all.

"It's a waste of time," said the receptionist. "She's not here. Your foreign friend must have got confused."

Konrad stepped forward and placed his hand on the counter. "This is not polite. You call me stupid because I am foreign. I must ask you—"

Cutting him off, Ben offered his biggest smile to the receptionist and said, "It would be so great if you could have a quick look at the computer. That would be really helpful."

"I suppose I can." The receptionist peered at her

130

screen and clicked her mouse, scrolling through the list of admissions. Then she shook her head. "I've looked through every patient who was admitted on Tuesday morning and there's only one head injury. That was a car crash."

"This is it!" Konrad waved his hands in the air. "This is her!"

"I'm afraid not," said the receptionist. "The names don't match. This woman is called Lucinda Smith."

"The computer is wrong," said Konrad. "Like he said, there is some confusion!"

"The computer is never wrong," said the receptionist.

Ben wasn't sure what to think. If Nina had been unconscious or confused, she might have been admitted under the wrong name. That explained why the police hadn't been able to identify her. But then why would she send a postcard signed with her own name?

Frank said, "What's happened to Lucinda Smith? Is she still here? In this hospital?"

"She's in ward six," said the receptionist. "But you can't visit her now unless you're immediate family."

"I am," said Frank. He turned and hurried

towards the door. Ben and Konrad jogged after him. The receptionist shouted something, but none of them could hear what she was saying, and then the door swung shut behind them, cutting off her voice.

There was a map of the hospital pinned to the wall. Ward six was on the second floor. Frank ran his finger along the map, tracing their route from here to there.

"This way," he said.

He was ready to go immediately, but Konrad stopped him. "I say goodbye now. I have to go back to work. And you don't need me no more."

"Bye, Konrad," said Ben. "Thanks for everything."

Frank nodded. "Yes, thank you. I'm very grateful for what you've done."

"No problem," said Konrad. "I hope your mother is safe. Say hello from me." He shook hands with both of them. Then he pulled a stubby pencil from his pocket. "You have paper? I give you my number. In case you need help again. Or maybe you need one good builder in London."

Ben had the map that Frank had printed for him. He tore it in two. Konrad wrote his number on one half and Ben scrawled his on the other.

They swapped halves and shook hands again. Then Konrad wished them luck and went to find his van.

Ben and Frank walked briskly down the long white corridor. They turned left, then right, and crossed a crowded hallway, packed with staff, patients and visitors. Ben wondered whether to say anything. Should he raise his doubts with Frank? No, maybe not. Better to see Lucinda Smith first. Find out who she really was.

Frank suddenly said, "Stay here."

"Where are you going?"

Frank darted away without answering. He crossed the corridor and went into a shop selling sandwiches, drinks and magazines.

Ben couldn't understand what Frank was doing. Did he really need to buy a sandwich at a time like this? And how was he going to pay for them? They had shared all their money back in London.

The air smelt stale and old. Two porters wheeled a woman past on a trolley. An old man in a flowery dressing gown shuffled alongside a tall, slender woman who might have been his granddaughter. A woman hurried towards the exit, already pulling a cigarette from its packet, ready to light up as soon as she emerged into the fresh air.

Ben hoped he'd never have to spend any time in hospital. Just being here made him feel ill. He imagined all the germs swirling through the air, breathed in and out by sick people, and wondered what diseases he was sucking into his own lungs.

Frank emerged from the shop with a large bunch of flowers wrapped in cellophane and tied with a red ribbon.

Ben said, "I thought you didn't have any money."

"I kept some."

"We were meant to share everything."

"Lucky I didn't," said Frank. "Otherwise I couldn't have bought these. Come on, let's go and find my mum."

28

Ben and Frank walked through ward six.

Looking at the faces of the patients in the beds, Ben could see nothing but pain and suffering. The overhead lights cast a yellowish glow which made people look even sicker than they were.

A nurse stopped them. "Can I help you?"

"We're looking for Lucinda Smith," said Frank.

"I'm afraid you can't see her."

"Why not?"

"These aren't official visiting hours. Only family are allowed now. Can you come back later?"

"I am family," said Frank. "I'm her son."

"She's never mentioned a son."

"Well, that's who I am."

The nurse peered at his face, searching for some resemblance between him and her patient, then shrugged her shoulders. "I suppose you'd better see her then." She pointed down a corridor. "Third door on the left. Don't stay too long, mind. She gets tired easily."

Frank thanked her. He and Ben hurried down the corridor. They reached the third door on the left. Someone had scrawled a name on a whiteboard in blue ink: LUCINDA SMITH.

They stood there for a moment, not wanting to go in, nervous of what they might find. Then Frank pushed the door and stepped inside. Ben followed him and shut the door behind them.

The only light in the small windowless room came from a dim bedside lamp. A TV was fixed on a bracket on one wall. There was a painting hanging on another wall, a few squiggles of scarlet against a yellow background. Poppies in a cornfield, perhaps, or a beautiful sunset.

A woman was lying on the bed with her face turned away from the door. Her head was wrapped in bandages. Her left leg and her right arm were held in place by metal splints. She was surrounded and supported by so many wires and tubes that she looked like a cyborg, half human and half machine, a brain and a body augmented by plastic and metal.

On the bedside table, there was a plastic jug half-filled with water, two empty glasses and a pile of magazines. Some old flowers drooped in a blue vase.

Frank spoke in a very low voice: "Mum."

She didn't answer.

He spoke a little louder: "Mum."

Still no answer.

Frank glanced at Ben and whispered, "Should I wake her up?"

"Don't ask me. She's your mum."

"I could just leave a note."

"If you want to."

"Or we could wait."

"Like I said, it's your choice."

Frank thought for a moment. "I think I should I wake her up."

He tiptoed round to the other side of the bed and leaned slowly down towards her face. Then he blinked. And straightened up again.

"This isn't my mum."

"Who is it?" said Ben.

"I don't know. I've never seen her before."

Ben hurried round the room and stood beside Frank. Together, they looked down at Lucinda Smith.

She was about fifty. She had dark hair, fine features and a long, thin nose. Her face was covered with half-healed cuts and mottled bruises. And she definitely wasn't Frank's mum.

29

Ben knew what they had to do. Get away from here. They were trespassing in a stranger's hospital room. If they were caught, they'd probably be arrested. And even if they weren't, they would be asked all kinds of awkward questions. Who are you? Where are your parents? Do they know you're here? He whispered to Frank, "Let's go."

"I want to stay here for a minute," said Frank.

"Why?"

"I just do."

"What if she wakes up?"

"She's on drugs," said Frank. "You can talk as loudly as you want and she's not going to wake up."

"But what if someone comes in? What if the nurse comes back? This is probably illegal. We're trespassing. We could be arrested."

"If you're scared, you can wait for me outside."

"I'm not scared."

"Then stay here."

Ben sighed. Of course he was scared, but he couldn't admit it. So he sat down on the one chair in the room, an uncomfortable armchair with soggy springs, and tried to think where he had gone wrong and what he had done wrong.

If he was a detective, searching for a missing woman, and he found himself in a hospital room with the wrong woman, what would he do? How would he find the right woman?

Evidence, thought Ben. That's the key to any case. Go through the evidence. Decide what's important and what's not.

He fished into his pocket and pulled out his list of questions. He ran through the list, checking what he had written against what he had learnt, hoping something would leap out at him, but he couldn't think of anything that he hadn't already thought a hundred times.

This is hopeless, he thought. I'm not a detective. I'm just a dumb kid who ran away from home.

His mum had been right. So had Frank's dad. Leave it to the professionals. They know what they're doing.

Should he give his list to the police?

No, they'd just laugh at him. Or, even worse, they'd pretend to be grateful. They'd thank him with patronizing smiles. Then they'd dump his list in the bin without bothering to read it.

And then he saw it.

The clue. The vital piece of evidence. The crack in the case.

When Pavel saw the photo of Nina, he recognized her immediately. So did Konrad.

But Lucinda Smith didn't look anything like Nina Fitzroy. No one would ever mistake one of them for the other.

Lucinda Smith had been injured in a crash and brought straight to the Bristol Royal Infirmary. But she wasn't the woman that Pavel and Konrad had seen.

So where was Nina?

He turned to his brother. "I've just realized something."

"Yeah? What?"

Ben explained what he had worked out. He told Frank about Pavel and Konrad, pointing out the contradictions in their stories. "They can't speak very good English, but they're definitely not stupid. So how could they have mixed up different women? Why did they say they recognized the photo?" He pointed at Lucinda Smith. "Who could mistake her for your mum? They don't look anything like one another. It just doesn't make sense."

Frank said, "What about the bike?"

"Which bike?"

"My mum's."

"What about it?"

"They've got it, haven't they?"

"I told you. They kept it in the garden."

"Let's go back to your builders and ask them to show it to me. If it's my mum's, we'll know she was the person in the accident. If it's not hers, then they mixed her up with someone else and this whole thing has been a complete waste of time."

"We don't have to go anywhere," said Ben. "I took a photo." He pulled out his phone and scrolled through the menus, searching for the picture, then turned the screen to face Frank. "Is that it?"

Ben expected that he wouldn't have to wait for an answer, because he was sure that the expression on Frank's face would tell him everything, but he was wrong. Frank didn't show a glimmer of emotion. He simply took the phone out of Ben's hand and studied the small screen for a few seconds, his face blank, his expression unmoved. Then he nodded. "Yes, that's it. That's definitely hers."

"Are you sure?"

"Of course I am. I know what my own mum's bike looks like."

"That's even stranger," said Ben. "Pavel and Konrad must have been telling the truth. Just like they said, they heard the crash and called 999. The ambulance picked her up and took her away. But it can't have come here, because it would have been logged on the computer. So where did it go?"

"A different hospital?" suggested Frank.

"They told Pavel and Konrad that they were coming here."

"Maybe they got diverted. Maybe they were sent to another accident and they picked up another patient and took them both to a different hospital."

"If that had happened, wouldn't there be a record on a computer?"

"There should be. If their system has been set up properly. We could go and ask that woman to take another look at her database."

"I don't think she'd help us."

"What about the driver?" said Frank.

"He drove off. Pavel tried to get his number plate, but he wasn't quick enough. I told you that already."

"Not the driver who hit her. The driver of the ambulance. We should find him. He must know what happened to her."

"How are we going to find him?"

"We're in a hospital, aren't we?"

Ben grinned. "Good point. Let's go." He started towards the door.

"Wait," said Frank.

"Why?"

"She should have these."

Frank pulled the old flowers from the vase and replaced them with the fresh ones.

They left the room and hurried along the corridor towards the exit. When they passed a rubbish bin, Frank lifted the lid and stuffed the dead flowers inside, snapping the stalks as he pushed them down.

30

They found Harmony and Kitkat at the front of the hospital and told them what had happened. Then the four of them went to the Accident & Emergency Department. An ambulance was parked outside. The driver was just opening the door and swinging himself down the ground.

Ben explained what they were doing.

"I wish I could help you," said the ambulance driver. "But I wasn't working last Tuesday."

"Do you know who was?"

"Haven't a clue. It's all rotas." The driver was just turning to leave when he saw the expression on Ben's face. It must have softened him, because he darted back. "I'll tell you what to do. Go to Mickey's. Ask for Sean. I'm pretty sure he was here last Tuesday morning."

"What's Mickey's?" said Ben.

*

Mickey's turned out to be a crowded café with steamed-up windows. Men and women in all sorts of different uniforms were sitting at the tables. There were doctors and nurses, policemen and policewomen, drinking big mugs of tea and eating plates piled high with eggs and toast and chips and beans.

Three men were sitting at a table near the door. They were wearing green uniforms with PARAMEDIC stitched into the material. Ben said, "Excuse me? I'm looking for a man who drives an ambulance. His name is Sean. Do you know him?"

"Everyone knows Sean," said one of the drivers. He pointed across the café to a small man with a neat black moustache who was sitting alone, hunched over a newspaper. He was wearing the same green uniform.

Ben, Frank, Harmony and Kitkat walked through the café to the moustached man. Ben said, "Excuse me? Are you Sean?"

The man lifted his head. "That depends."

"On what?"

"Who's asking. And why."

"My name is Ben. This is Frank, Harmony and Kitkat. We're looking for someone." Ben pointed at Frank. "His mother."

"What's her name?"

"Nina Fitzroy."

Sean shook his head. "I don't know her."

"Maybe you don't know her name," said Ben. He reached into his pocket and pulled out the photo of Nina. "But do you recognize her face?"

Sean peered at the picture for a moment, then shook his head again. "Never seen her before. Sorry."

"Were you working at the hospital last Tuesday morning?"

"I should think so. I usually work on Tuesdays."

"She was picked up in an ambulance. Were you the driver?"

"It's very possible," said Sean. "I was working on Tuesday and I drive an ambulance. But, like I said, I don't remember her. To be honest, I don't remember many of them. All the faces blur into one. It sounds bad, I know, but it's the truth. I must have been doing this job too long."

"She was riding her bike along Bradfield Avenue," said Ben. "She was hit by a car, then picked up by an ambulance. How can we find out who was driving the ambulance? And where they took her?"

"Bradfield Avenue," repeated Sean. Somewhere

deep in his mind, the name of the road had sparked a memory, but he wasn't sure what he was remembering or why it should have been memorable. "Let me look at that picture again."

Ben placed the photo on the table and flattened it out.

Sean stared at the picture for a minute. Then his expression changed. "I don't believe it. She's the runner."

"What do you mean?" said Ben. "What's a runner?"

31

Sean described how he and his co-driver had driven their ambulance to Bradfield Avenue and found a woman in the road.

"She was sitting up. There were a couple of builders with her. They were working on a house in the street and they'd heard the crash. They didn't speak much English, but they told us what they knew. I talked to the patient. I asked her to describe the accident, but she couldn't remember what had happened. She said she felt fine. She told me she didn't want any fuss. She'd hit her head, but there wasn't any bleeding and she didn't even have a headache. She even asked me if we'd give her a lift to work. I told her that wasn't a good idea. I said I couldn't force her to come to hospital if she didn't want to, but I explained the risks and she eventually agreed to come with us."

Frank said, "What are the risks?"

"Head injuries can be deceptive," explained Sean. "If you fall over and bang your head, you might feel fine at the time. You don't notice anything unusual. Nothing hurts. You carry on with your normal life. You walk home or go to work. An hour later, you get a headache. An hour after that, you collapse. And a few hours after that. . . Well, anything might happen. If you hit your head, you should always go to hospital and have proper tests. The brain is a delicate instrument. That's what I told your mum and, I'm glad to say, she was convinced."

"So where did you take her?" asked Ben.

"We came here," said Sean.

"To this hospital?"

"Yes."

"Then why wasn't she on the computer?"

"If you give me a chance, I'll tell you." Sean took a gulp of tea. "When we were in the ambulance, I asked her name, but she wouldn't tell me. I don't know if she was confused by the accident or annoyed about going to hospital, but there didn't seem much point pushing her. She had a little red rucksack. She kept a tight grip on it. I could have looked inside and found her diary or her phone, but I didn't want to prise it out of her hands."

Harmony said, "Did she ask you any questions about her injury?"

"Not that I can remember."

Ben said, "Did she say anything at all?"

"No, not really. She was very quiet."

"That's not like her," said Frank. "She normally talks all the time."

"We weren't together for long," said Sean. "Driving back to the hospital can't have taken more than ten minutes. We took her into A & E and I handed her over to a nurse. I went back to check on her about half an hour later, but she'd already upped and left."

"Where did she go?" asked Ben.

"I don't know. I wasn't there. According to the nurse, she'd met some friends and decided to leave with them. The nurse tried to persuade her to stay, but she didn't want to."

"She just walked out?" said Frank.

"Exactly."

Harmony said, "Had she been seen by a doctor?"

"No."

"I thought you said anyone with a head wound had to be checked by a doctor and given proper tests."

"That's what we advise."

"Why didn't anyone stop her?"

"It's a free country. No one has to stay in hospital if they don't want to. I'd advised her to stay. So had the nurse. But she chose not to."

"Who were these 'friends'?" asked Frank.

"I don't know. I wasn't there. I didn't see them."

"It doesn't make any sense," said Frank. "I know Mum's friends. If they found her in hospital, they'd tell me. Anyway, why would they take her out of hospital? Why wouldn't they wait for her to be seen by the doctors? Didn't they know she'd hit her head?"

"Those are all good questions," said Sean. "Unfortunately I don't know any of the answers. If I'd had a chance to talk to your mum's friends, I would have advised them of the risks. But I wasn't there. By the time I'd got back, she'd gone."

Ben said, "Could we talk to the nurse?"

"She won't tell you any more than me."

"We'd still like to talk to her. What's her name?"

"Elena."

"Do you have her phone number?"

"I don't," said Sean. "But she's working today. You'll find her in A & E."

32

Elena turned out to be a short, dark woman with brown eyes and a worried expression. "I'm very busy," she said. "Could you come back in an hour or two? I'll have time to talk to you then."

The Accident and Emergency Department was packed with people waiting to be seen by Elena and her colleagues. A teenage boy was holding a bloodstained bandage against his face. A pale, sweaty man clutched his belly and groaned. A red-faced baby screamed and wriggled in its mother's arms. A large family were arguing in loud voices, waving their arms and jabbing their fingers at one another; it was impossible to know which of them was ill.

"This won't take more than a minute," said Harmony.

"We're looking for a missing person," added Ben. "Sean said you'd be able to help."

"Sean? Who's Sean?"

"The ambulance driver."

"Oh, that Sean. How do you know him? And what's all this about? Who's missing?"

Frank explained about his mother.

"Yes, I remember her," said Elena. "She met some friends and left with them. I tried to persuade her to stay, but she insisted on leaving. I don't have the right to make someone stay in hospital against their wishes."

Frank said, "Who did she leave with?"

"I told you. Some friends."

"Men or women?"

"Both. They were a big crowd. Eight people, maybe ten. Very polite, very calm. One of them had cut himself with a knife. He'd been chopping vegetables, I think. The others had brought him here and now they were taking him home."

"Where did they live?" asked Frank.

"I don't know."

"What did they look like?" said Ben.

"Different."

"What do you mean?" said Frank. "Different to what?"

Elena suddenly smiled. "I shouldn't have said 'different'. That's the one thing they weren't. They were all dressed in the same clothes. Every one of them the same. Long yellow robes stretching almost to the floor. And on their feet, they were wearing sandals. As if they'd just walked off the beach."

"Like monks?" said Frank.

"Yes, I suppose they could have been a group of monks."

"And my mother knew them?"

"That's what she said. They were her friends."

"My mum doesn't have any friends like that."

"She said she did. She said she knew them. She said she wanted to leave with them. I suggested she stayed, but she was very insistent. She said she hated hospitals and she felt fine and she wanted to leave with her friends. And then they left." Elena glanced at her watch. "I'm very sorry, I'd better go. I wish I could help you more."

Ben said, "Do you keep the names and addresses of patients?"

"Of course we do," said Elena.

"So you'd know the name and address of the person who'd cut himself with a knife?"

"It'll be on the computer, yes. But we can't share that information."

"We're looking for his mother," said Ben. "She's

been gone for a week. No one knows where she went. Couldn't you just have a quick look at the computer and find their address?"

Elena shook her head. "I wish I could, but I can't. Patient details are strictly confidential. I wouldn't just get fired, I'd be prosecuted. Talk to the police. They might be able to help. Look, I'm very sorry, I have to go. Good luck. I hope you find your mum."

They thanked her and she hurried back to work.

They sat on a row of plastic chairs in the corner of the room. Kitkat leaned forward and said in a low voice, "What are we going to do now?"

They looked at Frank, expecting him to have an answer, but he didn't even appear to have heard what Kitkat said. He had reached into his rucksack and taken out his computer. Now he was staring intently at the screen and fiddling with the keys.

Ben felt like asking if this was the perfect moment to write an email. Can't you wait? he could have said. Don't you have more important things to worry about? Instead, he turned to Kitkat and answered her question. "We've got to find these 'friends', whoever they are."

"I know we do," said Kitkat. "The question is: how?"

"They sound pretty distinctive," said Ben. "Someone must have seen them. Someone must know where they came from or where they were going."

"Maybe someone did," said Kitkat. "But how are we going to find them?"

"Let's ask around. We should split up. Someone should talk to the other nurses and the doctors and see if they remember anything. Someone should talk to the receptionist at the front desk. And one of us should go back to Mickey's and talk to the police and the ambulance drivers." He stood up. "I'll do that."

"We don't need to talk to anyone," said Harmony. "We just need to get the address from the computer."

"And how do you suggest we do that?"

"We can't," said Harmony. "But the police can. We should call them and tell them what we've discovered. They can come here and check the computers and find out all about these friends or these monks or whoever they are."

"The police are useless," said Ben. "There's no point ringing them. They won't do anything. We've found out more than them in one morning – and we're just a bunch of kids."

"They might have been useless before," said Harmony. "But now they could do some good."

"Why will they be any better than they were before?"

"It's a risk worth taking."

"No, it's not," said Ben. "We should keep all this information to ourselves. We're making progress. We're finding things out. We're getting closer to the truth. We just have to keep going. Telling them will ruin everything."

"No, it won't."

"Yes, it will."

"No, it won't."

"Yes, it will."

"No, it won't."

"Yes, it will."

"Stop it," said Kitkat in a stern voice. "You've got to stop it right now. You're both being pathetic."

"Don't talk to me like that," said Ben. "I'm older than you."

"I know you are," said Kitkat. "You're both older than me. Which is why you shouldn't be behaving like little children. Anyway, it's not up to you. Only one person can choose what we do and that's Frank. She's his mum." She turned to her brother. "Frank?"

"What?" mumbled Frank. He hadn't really been listening to the conversation.

"What do *you* want to do?" said Kitkat. "Should we ring the police and tell them what we've discovered?"

Frank shook his head. "No, no, no. That would be a big mistake. We should just find those monks."

"There's only one problem," said Ben. "We don't know where they live."

"I do," said Frank.

While the others were arguing, Frank had been searching the internet. He tried all sorts of different words in different combinations.

monks india taunton
yellow robes taunton
vishnu taunton swami
bristol monk yellow
yellow yoga hospital monk
bristol taunton swami yoga
bristol yoga yellow robes

Finally he typed in:

indian bristol yellow robes

And there it was. An article from the *Bristol Evening News*, written two years ago, but archived for eternity on the internet.

33

The Evening News
The oldest independent newspaper in the South-west

THEY STOLE OUR DAUGHTER!

FAMILY ACCUSES POLICE OVER ALLEGED CULT KIDNAP

The family of a young Somerset woman have complained that their daughter is being held hostage by a secretive cult in Abbots Leigh – and the Bristol police are refusing to get involved.

"We just want to get our daughter home again," said Brian and Janet Foster from Shepton Mallet.

"Why won't anyone help us?"

Meredith Foster is a pretty nineteen-year-old girl. Until last summer, according to her mother and father, she didn't have any worries in the world. Her only interests were her little brother, her best friends and her job as a hairdresser in Frome. But now, if Brian and Janet Foster are right, she has joined a strange cult led by a mysterious Indian man known only as "the Tiger".

On Saturday 14 June, Meredith came to Bristol for the day with two close friends. As far as anyone knew, they were planning to go shopping.

That night, Meredith rang her parents and told them she wasn't coming home. She said she was staying with friends.

She didn't say who those friends were – or where she had met them.

On Monday morning, she didn't arrive at work. And on Tuesday, she told her parents she wasn't coming home at all.

Brian and Janet Foster went to Bristol to find their daughter. They tried to persuade her to come home with them to Shepton Mallet. But Meredith refused. "It was the saddest day of my life," remembers Janet Foster. "My own daughter looked straight through me. As if I was a stranger."

"I've got a new family now," Meredith told her parents. "I don't want to live with you. I want to stay with them."

Since then, Meredith has been living with a bizarre organization who occupy a large residence in Abbots Leigh. Various sources allege that this organization is a cult, led by the Tiger.

We have been unable to establish his real name – or where he acquired his extraordinary nickname.

According to neighbours, the Tiger is a middle-aged man of Indian origin. At least thirty people are said to be living with him in "the Ashram" – the name that they give to their home.

Young and old, men and women, the Tiger's followers wear distinctive long yellow robes and eat only vegetarian food. There have been reports of loud music and unexplained noises coming from the house late at night.

Brian and Janet Foster have begged the police to take action against the Tiger. They have talked to their vicar, their MP and various experts in Britain and the USA. But no one can help them.

"Our daughter must have been brainwashed," they told the *Evening Post*. "She says she's happy – but how can she be happy? She's living with a bunch of hippies. Why won't she come home?"

A spokesman for the police gave the following statement to *The Evening News*. "We have investigated reports from various sources, but we can find no evidence of a crime having been committed. Meredith Foster is nineteen years old. In two separate interviews, she has told the authorities that she is capable of making her own decisions about her life and we see no reason to disbelieve her. We can understand why her parents may be unhappy with the current direction of her life, but we have no right to interfere. This is a private matter between a young woman and her parents."

34

Frank let each of them read the article and study the small, grainy photo of Meredith Foster.

"It all makes sense," said Kitkat. "They kidnapped her."

Ben shook his head. "The nurse said she went willingly. She said they were her friends."

"Maybe they had a gun or a knife."

"She might have been confused," suggested Harmony. "She'd hit her head. Maybe she thought they were her friends."

"Maybe she thought she was in India," said Ben. "That would explain the postcard."

"Come off it," said Frank. He gestured at the dirty walls and the queue of patients waiting to be seen. "Does this really look like India?"

"I don't know. I've never been there."

"Well, I have. And I can tell you, it doesn't look anything like Bristol."

"So what do you think happened?"

"I think they're a cult and they kidnapped her. We should go to the Ashram and get her back again."

"Have you found the address?" said Ben.

"No."

"Then how can we go there?"

"We'll get a bus to Abbots Leigh," said Frank. "It's just the other side of the Clifton Bridge. I went there once with Mum. It's quite nice, actually. When we get there, we'll ask around. Someone will know where it is."

"What if they don't?"

"We'll go to every big house in the area and look for people in yellow robes and sandals."

They took one bus from the hospital to the bus station in the centre of town, then another to Abbots Leigh. The bus fares used up almost all their remaining money.

The bus took them over Clifton Bridge and up a long hill lined with large houses, then dropped them beside a pub called The George. There was a little shop next door, selling sweets and snacks and newspapers.

"I'll ask in the shop," said Ben. "You wait here."

He went into the shop. Kitkat followed him.

"I want a packet of crisps," she said.

"Go outside. Wait with the others."

"Please, Benjy. Won't you just buy me a packet of crisps?"

"We don't have enough money."

"I'm starving."

"You can't be. You had a big elevenses on the train."

"That was hours ago. It's tea time now and I didn't have any lunch. Please, Benjy, don't torture me. My tummy's so empty, it hurts."

"We have hardly any money left. Do you really think it's sensible to spend it all on crisps?"

"Yes."

"Fine." Ben grabbed a pack of crisps.

"I don't like cheese and onion," said Kitkat.

"What do you like?"

"Salt and vinegar. You know that."

"Whatever," said Ben. He discarded the cheese and onion, grabbed a pack of salt and vinegar, and went to the counter. "These, please."

There was a slim blonde girl behind the counter, wearing a scarlet baseball cap and a Chelsea shirt. She couldn't have been much older than Ben. She said, "Do you need a bag?"

"No, thanks."

Ben paid for the crisps with the last of his coins.

"Maybe you can help me," he said. "We're looking for a place called 'the Ashram'. Do you know it?"

"Why do you want to go there?" said the girl.

"We're looking for someone. We think she might be staying there."

"And you want to get her out?"

"If we can."

"Good luck. They're weirdos, those people. You know that?"

"What's so weird about them?"

"They're like a cult or something. They wear these strange yellow clothes. They come in here sometimes, but they never buy much."

She led Ben out of the shop and pointed up the road to the top of the hill. "You see those trees? Just the other side of them, you'll pass a little lane there on the right. Go down that for five minutes and you'll see a big black gate. That's them. That's the Ashram."

35

They walked up the hill.

Kitkat opened her crisps and offered them round. "These will make you fat. And give you a heart attack. So I don't suppose anyone wants one?"

To her disappointment, everyone did.

As the blonde girl had said, they soon came to some thick woods, then a narrow lane on the right.

"Down here," said Ben. "This way to the Ashram."

He was just about to lead the way down the lane when Frank stopped him.

"I think you should stay here."

"Why?" asked Ben.

"We should split up. You three stay here. I'll go into the Ashram on my own. If I don't come back in a couple of hours, you can call the police and they'll come and find me."

"That's crazy," said Kitkat. "Why do you want to go in there alone?"

"This whole thing is my responsibility. She's my mum. I'm the one who wants to find her. You shouldn't have to suffer for me."

"We're not going to suffer," said Ben. "We're just going to go in there and get her out again."

Frank shook his head. "You don't know what's going to happen in there. Religious cults are packed with strange people. They probably think the end of the world is coming. They might be planning to take poison together. Or blow themselves up. Or blow everyone else up. It's going to be dangerous. I don't want you to take the risk."

"We're the Misfitz," said Kitkat. "We do everything together."

"She's not your mum," said Frank. "You don't have to risk your life for her."

"But you're our brother."

"I'm your half-brother."

"Whatever," said Kitkat. "If you're going into the Ashram, I'm coming with you."

"But you don't have—"

"Stop it," snapped Kitkat. "I'm coming too. And that's that."

Frank looked at the others. "What about you guys?"

"I'm not staying here," said Ben. "I want to see inside the Ashram. I want to find your mum. Whether you like it or not, I'm coming with you."

"Me too," said Harmony.

"You know you don't have to," said Frank.

"We know," said Ben. "But we want to."

"Fine." Frank shrugged his shoulders. "Then let's go."

They walked down the narrow lane.

After a few paces, the dark woods surrounded them. Birds sang. Leaves rustled. Two cars passed, one driving in each direction. The drivers cast curious glances at the four children, but didn't stop or even slow down.

Just as they were beginning to wonder if they had taken a wrong turning, they came to a high brick wall, topped with shards of broken glass.

"This is it," said Ben. "I bet it is."

Kitkat said, "Why do they need such a high wall? And all that glass?"

"They must have something to hide," said Ben.

They walked along the curving wall and came to a pair of wrought-iron gates. Through the gaps in the gates, they could see a gravel driveway and overgrown hedges and rose bushes laden with flowers and a large house which was half-shielded from view. Through gaps in the trees, they could see a pair of well-proportioned windows, untrimmed wisteria cascading down the wall, the corner of a roof and a row of spindly chimneys.

Ben knew the gates would be locked, but he rattled them anyway, just to check. They didn't budge.

There was a small bell and a shiny brass plaque attached to the pillar on the right-hand side of the gate. A row of discreet letters on the plaque read MONTGOMERY HOUSE. Underneath, a second row of even smaller letters read PLEASE RING FOR ASSISTANCE.

Kitkat said, "Shall I ring it?"

The others looked at Frank. He nodded. Kitkat jabbed the bell. They couldn't hear the sound of ringing, but that was no surprise. If the bell worked, it would ring in the house, out of earshot.

They waited.

Nothing happened.

Kitkat rang the bell again and still nothing happened.

She rang it a third time, leaving her finger

pressed down for at least ten seconds, then turned to the others. "Maybe it's not working."

"It is," said Frank.

"How do you know?"

"Look."

36

A solitary figure was sauntering down the gravel driveway towards them. He had dark hair, cut very short, and a long, lean face. His high cheekbones accentuated the shadows around his eyes, which were sunk deep into his skull. He was wearing a yellow robe which reached almost to his ankles. With every step that he took, the end of the robe flapped up, lifting for a moment, revealing a pair of scarlet flip-flops on his feet.

"He's one of them," Kitkat whispered to the others. "He's wearing what she said they wore."

"We can see that for ourselves," said Ben. "There's no need for a running commentary."

When the skinny monk came closer, they could see he was wearing a narrow black cord around his neck, strung with two brown gems, which bounced across his chest as he walked.

Ben remembered the picture on the front of the

postcard. The Indian god with chubby cheeks and a radiant smile. He was wearing a long yellow robe. And he had a black cord hanging around his neck, strung with two brown gems.

Ben glanced at his brother, wondering what emotions must be running through his body, now he was so close to finding his mother. Hope? Panic? Joy? Terror? But Frank's face showed no sign of any emotion at all. He looked cool and calm and entirely unruffled, as if he had stopped at the gates to ask directions.

The man spoke with a strong Scottish accent. "Hello, my friends. How can I help you?"

They hadn't discussed who was going to do the talking and, for a moment, no one did.

The Scotsman said, "You did ring the bell, didn't you?"

"Yes, we did," said Frank. "We've come to see Nina Fitzroy."

"Who?"

"She's my mother. I think she's staying here."

"Nina, did you say? Nina Fitzroy?" The Scotsman shook his head and smiled, revealing perfect white teeth. "I'm sorry, my friend. You've come to the wrong place. I know everyone who stays here and we don't have a guest by that name."

"She went missing a week ago," said Frank. "We're trying to find her. It's very important. We think she might have hurt herself. Could I just come inside and have a look around? I'd like to see if she's here."

"I wish I could help you," said the Scotsman. "But that's simply not possible. This is a sacred place. A private place. A sanctuary devoted to silence and meditation. We don't allow visitors."

"I'm not a visitor. I don't want to stay. I won't steal anything or hurt anyone. I just want to look for my mother. It won't take more than a few minutes. Can't you let me come and look for her?"

"I'm sorry, you can't. Visitors are strictly forbidden. It's just a rule, I'm afraid. A silly rule. But we can't break it. I hope you find your mother." The Scotsman lifted his hands and clasped them together in front of his chest. "Go in peace, my friends." Then he turned and started back to the house.

Frank called after him: "Wait!"

"Yes?"

"She might call herself by a different name. Do you know a woman called Padma?"

"Padma," repeated the Scotsman. He nodded.

"There is a woman here by that name, yes. I can't claim great knowledge of her, but she's here."

"That's my mother," said Frank.

"I thought you said you were looking for Nina Fitzroy."

"She was given the name 'Padma' in India."

"Maybe this is a different Padma."

"It's her," insisted Frank. "I know it is. Did she arrive a week ago?"

"I'm not so sure," said the Scotsman. "She's been here a few days, I know that much, but I can't tell you exactly when she came."

"It would have been last Tuesday," said Ben.

"She came from the hospital," added Harmony.

"She had an accident," said Frank. "She was sitting in A & E, waiting to see a doctor, and she met some people. We don't know their names. We just know they were dressed like you. They were wearing yellow robes and sandals. We think they met her and brought her back here."

The Scotsman nodded. "Then you're right. That's Padma. She came from the hospital. If you say it was last Tuesday, I'll believe you."

Ben cheered and clapped his hands together.

Harmony cried out, "She's here!"

Kitkat jumped up and down on the spot. "We've

found her! We've found her! We've found Frank's mum!"

Only one person wasn't celebrating and that was Frank. If he was feeling elation, exhilaration or any other extraordinary emotions, he gave no sign of them. He simply said in a quiet voice, "I'd like to see her, please. Can you open the gates and let me in?"

"I'm sorry," said the Scotsman. "I told you before, this is a sacred place. A private place. No strangers are permitted. I can deliver a message if you like, but she won't receive it for a few days. She's on a retreat."

"What does that mean?" said Ben.

"It's a period of meditation and silence to renew and purify the body and soul. She'll be fasting. Chanting. Praying. Not speaking. Not reading. Avoiding all distractions. Simply spending time alone and in silence. Returning to the core of her being. I've just emerged from a retreat myself and, I can promise, nothing compares to the wonder of it. She will have seen into the depths of her soul and she will return to the world a new person. Full of knowledge. Full of happiness. Full of peace. Would you like to leave a message? I can arrange for it to be waiting for her when she emerges."

"I want to speak to her now," said Frank.

"You can't do that. She's specifically asked to be alone."

"I'm her son."

"You may well be, but you'll still have to wait until the retreat is finished."

"Why?"

"I've already told you. The retreat is her choice, her request. She doesn't want to be disturbed. Even by her own son."

Kitkat suddenly snapped. She could contain herself no longer. "Let us in!" she yelled. "Frank wants to see his mum! You've kidnapped her! Give her back!"

"That is a ludicrous suggestion," said the Scotsman, his voice suddenly filled with angry passion. "This is a very sacred house. No one would ever be brought here against their will."

"We'll call the police," said Harmony. "You'll have to let them in."

"You can do what you like," said the Scotsman. "But I can tell you this much for sure. Padma asked to go on a retreat. She wishes to spend two weeks alone and in silence. She doesn't want to be disturbed until the time is right to emerge. If you were a good son – if you really loved your mother – you would respect her wishes and leave her alone." He raised his hands and, just as he had done before, clasped them together over his chest. "Peace be with you, my friends." With that, he turned his back on them and walked briskly back to the house, his feet crunching on the gravel.

37

"He was strange," said Kitkat.

"He was hiding something," said Ben.

"How do you know?" said Harmony.

"Just the way he talked. And the way he looked."

"Maybe he was telling the truth," said Harmony. "He didn't have to tell us anything. He could have lied about 'Padma'. But he didn't. He told us she was here. He even admitted she came from the hospital. Maybe she really has gone on a retreat."

"If she had," said Frank, "why wouldn't she tell me?"

"She did tell you," said Harmony. "She sent you a postcard."

"That doesn't make any sense. If she really wanted to tell me something, she would have rung me or emailed me. She wouldn't send a postcard. Anyway, the postcard didn't tell me where she was.

The postcard told me where she *wasn't*. It said she was in India, remember?"

"Maybe she thinks she is."

"Do you think my mum's an idiot?"

"I didn't say that," said Harmony. "But strange things happen when you hit your head. She could be confused. She might have lost her memory. She might really think she's in India."

Frank said, "Have you been to India?"

"No," admitted Harmony.

"Well, I have. Twice. And I can tell you, India does not look like this." Frank gestured at the sights and sounds of the English countryside that surrounded them – the leaves, the branches, the birdsong, the breeze. "However hard my mum hit her head, she's not going to muddle up India and Abbots Leigh. She lived there for months. She studied yoga there. And she's not an idiot. No, I'll tell you what's going on. They've kidnapped her. Just like they kidnapped that girl in that article in *The Evening News*. They're a cult and they kidnap people."

Kitkat was staring at her brother with wide open eyes. She whispered, "What are we going to do?"

"Sneak in," said Frank. "Find my mum. And get her out of there."

"How can we sneak in?"

"I don't know."

"There might be another entrance," suggested Ben. "Maybe the wall gets lower at the back of the house and we can climb over."

"It's worth a try," agreed Frank.

"Let's split up," said Ben. "Two of us should walk round the entire wall and check for places to climb over."

"Why only two of us?" asked Harmony.

"They've got to open the gates sometimes. People have to come in and out. They need food. Maybe they'll go for a walk. Two of us should wait here and watch what happens when the gate opens."

"Who does what?" said Kitkat.

"I'll check the wall with Frank," said Ben. "You stay here with Harmony and watch the gates."

"That's so sexist!" cried Kitkat. "Why should we stay here just because we're girls?"

"You can come with me if you want."

"Yes, please."

"Fine. Frank, Harmony, you don't mind staying here, do you?"

They didn't.

38

Ben and Kitkat walked around the Ashram, searching for a gate or a door or a hole in the wall.

Walking along the road was easy. Walking through the forest was more difficult. They pushed through brambles, clambered over fallen tree trunks and scrambled up and down the sides of a deep ditch.

Ben waited for Kitkat to start complaining or ask for a rest.

"You see," he would have said. "It's not sexist. It's just sensible. You should have stayed behind and watched the gate. Pushing through brambles and jumping over tree trunks – that's boys' work."

To his disappointment, he never got the chance to give this speech, because Kitkat kept up with him all the way round and didn't utter a single word of complaint.

*

Frank and Harmony found a good hiding place. They squatted on a fallen tree, hidden from the road by a mesh of brown leaves and branches. They could see the gates. They would see anyone who came in or went out, but they wouldn't be seen.

Frank opened his computer, googled "Montgomery House" and found some information on a local history page.

The house had been built as a private residence by Edwin Arthur Montgomery, a Victorian entrepreneur who owned a fleet of cargo ships. When he died, his son inherited the house and the ships, and swiftly lost the lot, spending every last penny on wine, women and horses. Montgomery House was sold to a pair of sisters, Enid and Ethel Whittlestone, who converted it into a school.

During the First World War, the Whittlestones' school became a hospital for wounded soldiers. Enid died of influenza after the war. Ethel tried to run the school alone, but it was too much for her. Since then, Montgomery House had been a hotel, a training college for catering students and an old people's home. Six years ago, the last of the pensioners had been moved elsewhere and their home was put on the market.

Frank found the estate agent's particulars, which offered photographs of the interior and a floor plan of the whole house. From the land registry, he learnt the date on which Montgomery House had been sold and precisely how much was paid for it. But he couldn't discover who actually bought it.

Ben and Kitkat twice caught a glimpse of the house on the other side of the wall – they saw the line of the roof and the silhouette of some chimneys – but they didn't find a gate, a door, a hole, a ladder or any other way of breaching the high wall which ran round the entire property.

After about half an hour, they found themselves back where they had started, standing outside the gates. Nothing had changed. The birds were still singing. The breeze was still rustling the trees. And the gates were still shut.

They stared into the trees, searching for any sign of their brother or their sister.

A high-pitched whistle came from the trees.

"That's them," said Ben.

He and Kitkat left the road and plunged into the woods. There was another whistle, then another, guiding them towards their hiding place. It was a good one: they didn't see any sign of Frank or Harmony till they rounded the fallen tree and found them sitting astride the trunk.

Ben said, "What's happened?"

"Nothing," said Frank.

"What do you mean?"

"What do you think I mean? Fifteen fat green aliens came through the gate, followed by the Queen of Thailand, riding an elephant."

"There's no need to be sarcastic."

"There's no need to be stupid. If I say nothing's happened, then it's pretty obvious that nothing has happened."

"How about you?" said Harmony in a conciliatory tone. "What did you discover? Anything useful?"

"No," said Kitkat.

"There wasn't a back door or a hidden gate," said Ben. "The high wall never even dipped. Even with a ladder, we couldn't climb over it. The top is covered with broken glass."

"I don't understand," said Harmony. "Why do they need such good security?"

"Because they've got something to hide," said Frank.

*

They sat on the fallen tree, peering through the leaves and branches, watching the gates and waiting for someone to arrive or depart.

It was cold and gloomy. A brief downpour sprinkled them with water, but luckily didn't develop into a full-blown storm. They didn't have anoraks or umbrellas in their rucksacks.

Ben thought about school. Just about now, if they hadn't come to Bristol, they would be going home on the bus. When they didn't arrive at the house, their mother wouldn't worry immediately. She'd assume the traffic was bad and the bus had been delayed. She would probably wait for half an hour. Maybe forty minutes. Then she'd ring their phones. And then their schools. And discover that all of them were ill.

He warned the others to put their phones on silent.

Harmony dug into her rucksack and shared around the remnants of elevenses – a few squares of chocolate, half a cheese sandwich, two tangerines, a carton of orange juice and some lemonade. "We should save some of this," she said. "For emergencies." But they were so hungry and thirsty that they finished the lot.

When the food and drink was gone, they sat in

silence, watching the gates, waiting for something to happen. Birds cooed in the trees. A squirrel perched overhead, peering at them. A silver car drove past, but didn't stop.

Kitkat said, "We could play a game while we're waiting."

"I brought Scrabble," said Ben.

"Perfect!" Kitkat sat up, suddenly excited. Then she realized he was joking. "That's not funny."

"Sorry."

"Doesn't anyone know any good games?" Kitkat looked at the others. "How about I Spy? Who wants to play I Spy?"

No one did.

"Fine," said Kitkat. "Let's just sit here and do nothing. That'll be fun." She sighed despondently. "If only someone could help us."

"But who?" said Harmony.

"And how?" added Frank. "What could they do?"

"Someone with a helicopter could drop us inside," said Kitkat.

"You're a genius," said Ben. "Let's ring up one of our many friends who happens to own a helicopter."

Kitkat ignored him. "Someone with a bulldozer could smash down the wall."

Ben said, "Why don't we just knock it down with a grenade launcher? I think I've got one in my rucksack."

Kitkat carried on ignoring him. "Someone with an ice cream van could ring on the bell and say they were selling ice creams and when everyone came out to buy one, we could sneak inside."

"Wait a second," said Ben. "I know who might be able to help."

39

They walked down the hill to The George.

Ben could see a white van parked outside the pub. A stocky man was sitting in the driver's seat. "That's him!"

Konrad was already swinging himself out of the van and hurrying up the hill. When he reached them, he shook hands with Ben and Frank. "Hello, my friends. It is very good to see you again."

"Thanks for coming so quickly," said Ben.

"No problem. As soon as I get your call, I jump in van." Konrad turned to the girls. "So this is your sisters, yes?"

"This is my sister, Harmony," said Ben. "And my half-sister, Kitkat."

"She's my half-sister," added Frank. "And she's my stepsister."

"I don't understand," said Konrad. "You are sisters or not sisters?"

"I've got the same mum as him and her," said Kitkat. "And the same dad as him. But I have a different mum to him and a different dad to her and him."

"This is worse and worse," said Konrad. "Who is who? Which is which?"

"Ben and I have the same mother and father," said Harmony. "When they got divorced, our mother married Frank's father, so he became our stepbrother. And then they had Kitkat together, so she's our half-sister. It's very simple, really."

"It is not simple," said Konrad. "It is very, very complicated. I am absolutely confused. Why do you not just have one mother and one father like everybody else?"

"I'll draw you a diagram," said Ben. "That's the easiest way to explain how our family fits together."

"But not now." Frank was impatient to get going. "When we've found my mum, you can draw as many diagrams as you want."

"Follow me," said Konrad. "Your limousine is waiting."

Konrad opened the back door and ushered Frank, Harmony and Kitkat into the van. They had to share the windowless space with a few old bags of tools, some lengths of timber and a lot of dirt.

Ben pointed up the hill and explained where they needed to go. He advised Konrad what to do and what to say. Then he clambered after the others.

"Last chance," said Konrad. "You can say no. We can ring police. You don't have to do it like this."

"We want to," said Ben.

"No problem." Konrad lifted his left arm and glanced at the cheap digital watch clasped to his wrist. "You sure you want nine? Not eight? Or seven?"

"Nine is fine," said Ben. "We need enough time to find her."

"Good luck," said Konrad. "I wish you well."

He slammed the door, then walked round to the front of the van and climbed into the driver's seat. He knocked on the wooden board that divided the front from the back and shouted: "Everyone is good?"

"Ready for action," Ben yelled back.

"Then we go!"

Konrad started the van and accelerated up the hill.

In the back, they were thrown off-balance.

Harmony fell against the back doors, Kitkat banged her head against the wall and Frank slipped over a bag of tools, falling forward on to his hands and knees.

Ben whispered, "What happened? Anyone hurt?"

"I'm fine," hissed Harmony.

"Me too," said Frank.

"Me three," said Kitkat.

They squatted on the floor and held on tight.

This is it, thought Ben. No turning back. We're trespassers now. We're breaking the law.

He glanced at the others, wondering how they were feeling, but he could barely see their faces in the gloom.

There hadn't been much time for discussion, but they had made a simple plan. They would get into the house. They would find Nina. They would get out again.

They had debated whether to split up. Should they divide into two teams? Should one or two of them stay outside, coordinating the search, communicating with the others by phone? But they finally decided to stick together. All for one and one for all.

*

Ben felt the van slowing down, then changing direction. He knew where they were going. They had reached the brow of the hill. Now they were turning down the little lane. Walking had taken them almost a quarter of an hour, but the van did the same distance in two or three minutes.

Ben heard the sound of the door opening. Then footsteps. Then silence for a long time. He knew what was happening. Konrad had rung on the bell and was waiting for the Scotsman to come and talk to him.

Just as Ben was beginning to wonder if anyone would ever answer the bell, he heard the sound of voices. One was Konrad's. The other belonged to a woman. The Scotsman must have swapped duties with someone else.

From his hiding place in the back of the van, Ben couldn't hear every word that was spoken, but he could distinguish enough scraps of dialogue to glean what was happening.

"I am here to mend pipes," said Konrad. "Will you show me to boiler, please?"

The woman asked who had called him.

"I don't know," said Konrad. "They talk to head office. They say they have problem with boiler. Head office ring to me and say to mend your boiler. Can you open gates and let me inside?"

The woman asked another question which Ben couldn't hear.

"First I must see boiler," replied Konrad. "Then I tell you problem."

"I haven't heard anything about any problems with the boiler," said the woman. "But I suppose you'd better come in."

Konrad climbed into the front of the van and slammed the door. He started the engine and drove through the gates.

Ben could hear the tyres rattling against the gravel drive. The van shook from side to side, then stopped with a sudden lurch.

"Ready?" hissed Ben.

Everyone was.

Footsteps pounded on the gravel. The back door swung open. Light flooded in. They could see nothing except the silhouette of a tall man.

"She's coming," whispered Konrad. "Go this way."

He ushered them out of the door and round the side of the van, shielding them from the woman's gaze.

Ben led the way. Kitkat and Harmony came next. Frank was last. They sprinted across the gravel towards the house.

40

Ben could see a dark doorway. He knew he had to get inside. If the woman saw them, all was lost. On the other side of the door, they would be hidden from her inquisitive eyes.

He turned the handle. The door opened. He darted inside, waited for the others to follow him, then swung the door shut and closed it with a click.

He knelt on the cold stone floor and peered through the keyhole. He could see Konrad standing by the white van. A moment later, a woman joined him.

Perfect timing. She hadn't seen them.

The woman was dressed in the same uniform as the Scotsman. She was wearing sandals, a long yellow robe and two beads strung around her neck. Her long black hair was pulled back from her face and tied in a single braid which hung down her back.

Ben couldn't hear them, but he could guess what was being said. The woman would ask Konrad to wait with his van while she went to find someone who knew about the boiler. She would quickly discover that no one had called a plumber. And then. . .

That was Konrad's business. He could look after himself. He would make up some story – he'd got the address wrong, perhaps, or he needed to go back to head office immediately – and find a way to get out of the Ashram. Then he would drive back to Bristol and wait for their call.

They had promised to ring him as soon as they found Nina. He would come back and collect them. If they hadn't contacted him by nine o'clock that night, he would ring the police.

Ben pushed himself to his feet.

It was time.

They were in.

Now they just had to find Nina.

He whispered to Frank, "Map?"

"Sure," said Frank.

He summoned the estate agent's details on his computer. They gathered round and peered at the screen, trying to work out where they were. The floor plan showed the shapes of the rooms, the entrances and exits, and the locations of the staircases. But there's a big difference between looking at a miniature map and stepping through the door of a strange house.

When Konrad drove through the gates, he had avoided the front door of Montgomery House. If he had stopped there, anyone who happened to be looking through the front windows would have seen what happened. Instead, he parked the van beside a one-storey annex attached to the side of the house.

They found the annex on the floor plan.

They were standing at one end of a long, narrow corridor with whitewashed walls. Anoraks and overcoats hung from pegs. Ten or twelve pairs of black rubber boots were arranged in a neat line and a bundle of umbrellas squatted in a black bucket. There was a wooden door to the left and another on the right.

According to the map, the left- and right-hand doors led to small self-contained rooms. If they went straight on, they would enter the main body of the house.

They had agreed to check the ground floor first. If Nina was a prisoner, Frank had said, she was probably being held in a basement. Why? Because basements usually just have one door, so they're easy to lock. You can't escape through the window, because basements don't have windows. And no one can hear your screams.

"Let's check these two rooms," whispered Ben. "Then find the cellar."

He opened the left-hand door and stepped into a small windowless room filled with cardboard boxes, old coats, dusty books, jam jars, a filing cabinet, a wooden chest of drawers and all kinds of other junk. But no prisoners.

He stepped out, closed the door and opened the other one. This room was smaller and neater. The walls were lined with shelves and each shelf held a different type of food. It looked like the storeroom for a shop or a restaurant. There must have been ten bulging sacks of rice, fifty packets of pasta, fifty more pots of jam and a couple of hundred big plastic packets of dried beans and dried lentils and dried chickpeas. Then there were the tins, hundreds of them, neatly stacked in rows three deep. Tinned peas, tinned spinach, tinned sweetcorn, tinned carrots, tinned mushrooms, tinned tomatoes – enough to feed five thousand people.

"I'm hungry," said Kitkat. "Are there any crisps?"

She scoured the shelves, but there wasn't any junk food. No crisps, no sweets, no chocolate. Just tins and jars which would last a year or two.

"They're preparing for a siege," whispered Frank. "They probably have guns and bombs hidden here too. They're going to barricade themselves in the house and shoot anyone who comes near."

"Maybe they just buy in bulk," replied Harmony. "It is much cheaper."

"Don't be naïve," said Frank. "Haven't you heard of Waco?"

"No. What's Waco?"

"It was a siege in Texas. The FBI invaded a ranch where—"

"We're wasting time," interrupted Ben. "If you want to stay here and talk about Waco, that's fine. But I'm going to find the cellars."

41

They looked at the floor plan on Frank's computer once more, plotting their route, then stepped out of the storeroom and walked slowly and carefully along the corridor that led deeper into the house.

Ben knew what the others were like. They could waste hours arguing about who should go first and who should go last and why it was unfair and what would be fair. Well, they didn't have hours to waste. Better just to make a decision. Without saying a word to anyone, he set off down the corridor at a quick march.

To his relief – and surprise – they followed him without complaint or protest, taking their positions as if they had already been agreed. They went in single file, Ben first, then Kitkat and Harmony, and Frank at the back.

The air was cool. The house was quiet. The

blank white walls reminded Ben of a school or a hospital.

This place *was* a school, he remembered. And a hospital, years ago, back in the First World War. Maybe no one had bothered changing the colour of the walls since then.

There was a strange smell in the air. Strong and sweet. Ben was sure he'd smelt it before, but he couldn't remember where or when. He sniffed a few times.

"Curry," whispered Harmony.

Ben turned round. "What?"

"The smell."

"How do you know?"

"I know what curry smells like."

"Shh!" Kitkat put her finger to her lips.

They listened in silence.

Kitkat was right. Now they could all hear them.

Footsteps. Getting louder. Someone was coming.

Ben gestured to the others. Back! Back! Go back the way we came!

They went fast, Frank first, then Harmony, Kitkat and Ben. Their feet scuffed on the stone floor, making some noise, but they didn't have time to worry about that.

Frank was the first to reach the two doors. He could have gone left – into the food store. Or right – into the junk room. Or straight ahead – outside. Turn right, Ben wanted to say. Please turn right. He wanted to shout at his brother, but he knew he couldn't make any noise.

Frank opened the door on the right and darted inside. The others followed him, one by one, and then Frank swung the door shut again. They stood there, breathing heavily, listening.

The footsteps were coming closer.

Ben looked at the others. He could see panic in their eyes. He wondered if he looked like that too and decided that he probably did. Up to now, he hadn't felt anything worse than a few butterflies in his stomach, but this was different. They were trespassing in a strange house. If they were caught, anything might happen. Anything at all.

The footsteps stopped.

A handle rattled.

A door opened.

But not this door.

Whoever he or she might be, the owner of the footsteps went into the storeroom. She or he came out again a moment later, closed the door and walked away.

The footsteps faded.

The house was quiet.

Harmony sighed. Ben grinned. Kitkat whispered, "We were so lucky."

"Luck had nothing to do with it," whispered Ben. "Frank chose the right door, that's all. If he'd gone through the other one, we'd have been caught."

"It was just a guess," said Frank. "A lucky guess."

Ben said, "Once more?"

The others nodded.

Ben opened the door. He looked both ways. There was no one to be seen.

They walked along the corridor in the same formation: Ben then Kitkat then Harmony then Frank. They retraced their route, stopping often, listening for footsteps, but they couldn't hear anyone or anything.

A narrow flight of steps led upstairs to the first floor. They would go that way later, once they'd checked the rest of this level.

According to the floor plan, there were three different staircases in the house. These ones, the smallest and the narrowest, would once have been used by the servants. That was what Frank said, anyway, when he was studying the floor plan. He didn't explain why he knew so much about old houses, but he sounded so confident that the others believed him.

There was a door to the left and a door to the right and an open archway at the end of the corridor, leading to the hallway and the front door and the large reception rooms.

Ben reached for the left-hand door.

"That one," hissed Frank, pointing to the right.

But it was too late. Ben had already opened the wrong door.

42

Later, when they were discussing what had happened, Ben claimed it hadn't been his fault. Everyone gets confused, he said. Everyone messes up their left and right. And I had to remember the map at the same time. Which was tiny. And upside down. You can't blame me for opening the door on the left rather than the door on the right.

But that was later. Now, he didn't have time to think about left or right, let alone justify how he had muddled them up. As soon as he opened the door, he found himself standing in the entrance to a wide room with whitewashed walls. There was an overpowering smell of sweet, strong, spicy curry. Gleaming silver appliances lined the walls – three big fridges and a huge oven and a hob with eight gas burners.

Two men were standing on the other side of a

long white work surface. One was tall and thin. The other was short and fat. They had red faces and shaved heads. They were wearing white aprons and holding large knives with long blades.

If the men had been facing in the opposite direction, Ben might have dodged backwards and closed the door, hoping to get out of the kitchen without being noticed. But both men were staring directly at him.

For a moment, no one spoke. The men stood very still, their knives poised. Then the taller of them said, "Hello. Who are you?"

Ben knew he had to say something, but he didn't want to tell them the truth, so he grabbed a name from his memory and said, "I'm looking for Meredith."

"Meredith? Who's Meredith?"

"Meredith Foster," said Ben.

"Who?"

"I know," said the other man, the smaller one. "He means Merry."

"That's her," said Ben. "Merry."

The tall man nodded. "Oh, sure. Merry. I didn't even know she was called Meredith. You're her brother, aren't you?"

"Yes." Ben didn't have any idea where this might

lead him, but he sensed it might offer a way out. He said, "I've come to visit her."

"She's told me all about you. How's the football?"

"It's great, thanks."

"Scored any goals recently?"

"A few."

"She's very proud of you. You know that, don't you?"

"Yes."

"She'll be really pleased to see you. Does she know you're here?"

"Not yet," said Ben.

The tall man glanced at a large clock on the wall. "She'll be doing her karma tasks right now," he said. "Then there's silent meditation from five till seven. I'm very sorry, but you won't be able to see her till she's finished. Didn't she tell you what time to come?"

"I'm early," said Ben. "But it doesn't matter. I don't mind waiting."

"Why don't you go and sit in the Serenity Room. We don't have a television, but you'll find some books there. And games, too. Do you want me to show you where it is?"

"Don't worry," said Ben. "I'll find it. Thanks for your help."

"My pleasure," said the tall cook. "Peace be with you."

The smaller man put down his knife and clasped his hands in front of his chest. "Peace be."

"Bye," said Ben and closed the door.

They held a whispered conference in the corridor.

Kitkat said, "How did you know what to say?"

"I didn't. I just remembered her name from that article. It was the first thing that came into my head."

Harmony said, "Why didn't you ask about Frank's mum?"

"I thought it was better not to. They'd know we're looking for her. Now they'll just think Meredith's brother is here."

"Till they talk to her," said Frank. "And that Scottish guy remembers us. Then they'll know exactly what's going on."

"I had to say something!"

"Forget it. We don't have time to waste. Let's go back to Plan A."

Kitkat said, "What's Plan A?"

"Opening the right door."

"I'm sorry," said Ben. "I mixed up my left and

right. I'd been looking at the map upside down and I couldn't—"

"I said forget it. Let's just get going."

"Sure." Ben crossed the corridor and opened the other door, the one that he should have opened first. This time, he found exactly what he had expected to see: a rickety flight of stairs leading down into the darkness.

There was a small white switch on the wall. Ben pressed it. A bare bulb flickered into life, lighting the way. He could see dirty walls and a spider's web and another door, down at the bottom of the staircase, secured with a single rusty bolt. A good place to keep a prisoner.

He walked carefully down the stairs. They creaked and wobbled with every step. The creaks didn't matter – he was sure no one could hear him down here – but he didn't like the wobbles. If a step snapped, he'd pitch forward and break his neck.

Kitkat followed close behind him. Then Harmony. And finally Frank, who pulled the door shut after himself.

43

The cellar was a single enormous room, lit by two bare bulbs, dangling from the ceiling. Strange shadows lurked in the corners. There was a mild smell of decay, as if someone or something had died down here, a long time ago, and gradually rotted away.

A long wine rack filled one wall, home for a thousand bottles. It now held nothing but a bundle of twigs, a rolled-up newspaper and an old black umbrella.

Junk had been piled against the opposite wall: cardboard boxes, battered suitcases, rusty tools, old rope, a mattress, some pillows, black bin bags filled with clothes, the whole lot coated with a thick layer of undisturbed grime.

But there was no sign of Nina or any other living creature.

"She's not here," said Kitkat in a quiet voice.

Ben scuffed the floor with his foot, kicking up a cloud of dust. "No one's been down here for years."

He glanced at his brother, expecting to see some sign of depression or defeat, but Frank was already reaching for his computer, planning what they should do next.

"She'll be upstairs," said Frank, searching for the floor plan on his computer. "They've probably locked her in the attic. That's the other logical place to keep a prisoner."

"Why?" asked Harmony.

"You're high up, so you can't escape out of the window. Unless you're an athlete or a mountain climber, and my mum isn't." Frank found the floor plan and checked their route. "We should go back to the servants' stairs. They'll take us up to the top floor and then we can search all the rooms in the attic."

Ben said, "What if she's not there?"

"Then we'll search the rest of the house. She's got to be somewhere." Frank put his computer in his rucksack and slung it over his shoulders. "Let's go."

There was a sudden rustling sound from the far end of the room.

"What was that?" hissed Kitkat.

"Rats," said Frank.

Kitkat took a step closer to Harmony. "I don't like this place."

"You don't have to worry about rats," said Frank. "They don't want any trouble. They only care about food and you're much bigger than their average snack."

"I'm scared," said Kitkat. "I want to go home." Frank might have been trying to reassure her, but his little lecture had actually had the opposite effect.

Harmony put her arm around her little sister. "Don't worry, we'll be fine. If there are really any rats here, Ben will fight them off. Won't you, Benjy?"

"Of course I will."

"No, he won't," said Kitkat.

"I will."

"How?"

"Like this." Ben darted forward and pulled the umbrella from the wine rack. "Come out 'ere, Monsieur Rat," he cried in a ripe French accent and lunged towards the end of the cellar, holding the umbrella like a rapier. "En garde! Touché! I am waiting, Monsieur Rat! I am ready for you, Monsieur Rat! Will you come and fight me?"

Kitkat giggled. "I think you've scared him off."

Ben darted forward, sweeping his umbrella-sword back and forth. "Are you scared, Monsieur Rat? Huh? Come on, Monsieur Rat! Show yourself! Come and fight!"

He was answered by the loud peal of a bell.

Ben froze. So did the others. They stood very still and listened to the bell, which went on and on and on, resounding through the house.

As abruptly and unexpectedly as it had started, the bell stopped.

"What was that?" whispered Kitkat.

"A bell," answered Ben.

"I know it was a bell. I'm not stupid. But what did it mean?"

"It might be an emergency signal," said Frank. "It probably tells everyone that there are intruders in the house. The Scottish guy or the cooks must have alerted the others and they're coming to get us."

"Let's hide here," said Harmony. "They won't think of looking in the cellar."

"Of course they will," said Frank. "It's the first place they'll look."

Directly above them, the floorboards thumped and rattled. Someone was walking over their heads.

With each step, a little cloud of dust puffed from the ceiling and fluttered down to the floor.

No, not just one person. Two... Three... Five... An army of footsteps paced across the wooden floor above them.

Ben tried to interpret the sound of the footsteps. What could he learn from them? What did they tell him about what was happening above his head? There were several people, he knew that much. At least five and maybe more. Were they running? Or walking? Were they gathering together in one big group? Or dividing up and heading to different parts of the house?

From what he could hear, he got the sense that all the footsteps were heading in the same direction. They sounded purposeful and steady rather than panicked. Not like guards hunting for intruders. More like hungry people hurrying to the dining room for lunch.

He pulled out his phone and looked at the display.

"It's five o'clock," he whispered. "The cook said there's silent meditation from five till seven. That's what the bell means. It's summoning them to silent meditation."

"How do you know?" said Harmony.

"I don't. I'm guessing. But I bet I'm right."

"Let's find out," said Frank. "Let's go upstairs and have a look at their silent meditation."

Kitkat stared at her brother in amazement. "Have a look? Why would we want to do that?"

"My mum might be there."

"I thought you thought she was locked up."

"That Scottish guy said she was on a silent retreat. If you're on a silent retreat, you do silent meditation."

"You mean he was telling the truth?"

"I have no idea," said Frank. "But I think Ben must be right. Silent meditation has started. That's what the bell meant. If you want to stay here or go home or do anything else, you can. I don't mind. Do what you want. But I'm going to go and see if my mum is there."

"We're meant to do everything together," said Kitkat. "We're the Misfitz, remember? All for one and one for all! You can't just go off and do things on your own."

"Then come with me," said Frank.

Kitkat folded her arms and gave her brother a strong stare. "That's not very democratic."

"I'm not interested in democracy," said Frank. "I just want to find my mum."

44

They followed their own footsteps in the dust across the cellar's floor to the rickety staircase.

Ben went first. At the top of the stairs, he opened the door just enough to expose a slim crack of light.

He waited and listened.

The house was quiet. He could hear nothing but his own breaths. Someone might be poised on the other side of the door, silent and stealthy, ready to pounce, but he'd have to take that risk. He couldn't stay here for ever. He opened the door all the way and stepped out.

The corridor was empty.

He could hear a sound now, a distant voice, coming from the main body of the house, but it was so quiet that he couldn't even tell whether the speaker was a man or a woman, let alone what they were actually saying.

He beckoned to the others. They joined him. Frank switched off the light in the cellar and closed the door.

Ben touched his ear, telling them to listen. Then he pointed down the corridor and raised his eyebrows.

They understood what he meant. One by one, they nodded. Yes, you're right, let's go that way.

They went in single file, Ben first, then Kitkat and Harmony, and Frank at the back. They walked slowly and cautiously, testing the floorboards with every step. Ben was sure someone would come round the corner and bump into them, but they didn't meet anyone. The rooms and corridors appeared to be empty.

We're being stupid, thought Ben. We're walking through a strange house in broad daylight. We're going to get caught. This is dumb.

But he didn't want to turn round or run away. Not now. Not yet. Not when they were so close.

With every step that they took, the voice grew louder. It belonged to a man, they could hear that now, and he was talking calmly and quietly and constantly, pausing only to take a breath. He might have been teaching a lesson or reading a poem.

When his voice rose, putting a stress on a particular word or phrase, they could hear a fragment of what he was saying, and then his voice fell away, disappearing into an inaudible mumble.

"What you need. . . Take one step. . . You can be free. . . Love is all. . . Come in peace. . . Dreams. . . Your home is here. . . Nothing else. . . My heart is yours. . . Hope. . . Hold each breath. . . My love for you. . ."

They followed his voice through the house. Ben paused at every doorway and intersection, listening for footsteps, but they didn't meet anyone. A few pictures hung on the white walls, black and white photographs of temples and colourful paintings of Indian gods. They passed the front door, which was closed, and a pleasant room filled with sunlight and armchairs, and then they found the source of the voice.

They could hear every word now. The speaker had a strong Indian accent. He was saying: "Breathe deeply. Hold your breath for a moment. Repeat your mantra to yourself. When any thoughts come to mind, observe them. Then let them drift away from you."

The door was open. Ben stepped into the room, followed by Frank, Kitkat and Harmony.

Right in front of them, there was a man sitting on a large squishy yellow cushion. He had his back to the Misfitz, so they couldn't see his face, but they could tell from the movement of his back and shoulders that he was talking.

He's the Tiger, thought Ben. He must be. He's the leader of the cult and he's talking to his disciples.

Two men sat on the Tiger's right and two women sat on his left. Ben could only see the backs of their heads and the outlines of their bodies, but he was sure he recognized one of the men: he was the skinny Scotsman who had turned them away at the gates.

Facing the Tiger and the Scotsman – and facing the Misfitz too – thirty or forty people were sitting on the floor.

There were roughly equal numbers of men and women.

They were barefoot. Their legs were crossed. Their upturned hands were resting on their knees.

Most of the men had shaved heads and most of the women had long hair, but all of them were dressed identically in yellow robes. And each of them had the same piece of jewellery hanging around their necks: a pair of brown gems strung on a black cord.

If their eyes had been open, they would have

seen the Misfitz immediately. But their eyes were shut.

They were breathing deeply and rhythmically, following the Tiger's instructions and concentrating all their attention on their meditation.

And there was Nina.

No doubt about it. That was her.

She was sitting near the back of the group. Apart from her face, she looked no different to the others. She had the same clothes, the same beads, the same posture and the same closed eyes.

Ben thought quickly. What could they do? How could they rescue Nina and get her out of this crowded room without being caught? The answer was obvious: they couldn't. Four kids against forty adults – it was impossible. They would have to be cunning. No one had seen them yet. If they crept out of the room now and found a good hiding place, they could wait till Nina was alone and then whisk her away.

These thoughts flashed through his mind in a moment.

In the same moment, Frank took two quick steps into the room and shouted at the top of his voice:

"MUM!"

45

No one moved.

Forty people stayed exactly as they were, sitting on the floor, legs crossed, eyes closed.

They must have heard Frank.

Ben *knew* they had. He saw one twitch, another turn her head, a third lurch backwards as if she'd received an electric shock. But not one of them opened their eyes.

What was wrong with them?

Were they deaf? Or drugged?

If they were, Nina was too. She didn't move either. She must have heard her son. It was extremely likely that she had even recognized his voice. But she didn't open her eyes to see where he was. Her eyelids didn't even quiver.

Then one man turned his head and looked at the Misfitz. The chanter. The speaker. The head of the cult.

Ben knew immediately why he was called the Tiger.

His eyes.

His blazing eyes.

He was a chubby little man with bushy eyebrows and a mop of curly black hair parted in the middle. He was wearing the same uniform as his disciples: a long yellow robe and a pair of brown gems hanging around his neck. His feet were bare. His cheeks were clean shaven. And his big brown eyes glowed like hot coals in the heart of a fire.

Harmony didn't move. Nor did Kitkat. Just like Ben, they stood very still, rooted to the spot, staring into the Tiger's eyes, captivated by the strength of his gaze.

But Frank. . .

Frank knew what to do.

He darted forward, heading for his mother.

Four people surrounded the Tiger – two men on his right and two women on his left – and they must have been his bodyguards, because they didn't take part in the meditation, but kept their eyes open at all times, watching for danger. They were alert and fit and fast. As soon as Frank moved, the four of them spread out, trapping him like a net.

Frank tried to dodge them, but he wasn't quick enough.

The Scotsman was the closest. He reached out and grabbed Frank with both arms.

Frank writhed and kicked.

The Scotsman must have trained as a soldier or a policeman. With one quick movement, he whirled Frank round and twisted his arm behind his back, then bundled him out of the room. By the time Frank caught a breath and shouted for help, he was already halfway down the corridor.

The other three attendants ushered Ben, Harmony and Kitkat after their brother. If they had struggled and fought, they might have been able to escape. One of them would have done, anyway, even if the others were captured. Kitkat could have darted forward and thrown herself at Nina. Or Ben could have sprung backward, darted up the main staircase and found a hiding place in the depths of the house. But that would have meant deserting the others and no one wanted to be a deserter. Better to stay together.

The Scotsman marched Frank to the back of the house and released him into a small room with a wooden table and four chairs and a window looking out on a wide green lawn bathed in sunlight.

As soon as Frank was free, he whirled round. "Get out of my way! Let me out of here! I want to see my mum!"

"We've been through this already," said the Scotsman. "She can't see you. She's asked to be alone."

"You're lying! You've kidnapped her!"

"Don't be stupid. We're not criminals. She's here because she wants to be here."

"Liar!"

Frank threw himself forward, trying to push past and get out of the door, but the Scotsman was wider and taller and stronger than he was – and much more experienced too. He easily shoved Frank back into the room, then nodded to the other guards. "Bring them in."

They pushed Ben, Harmony and Kitkat into the room after their brother.

The Scotsman could have closed the door and locked them inside, but he didn't bother. He just stood in the doorway, a human blockade, securing the room with his own body.

Frank was wild-eyed and desperate. He wanted to hurl himself at the Scotsman, but he knew there

226

was no point. He couldn't get past. He paced backwards and forwards, casting furious glances at the Scotsman, then looking at Ben and Harmony and Kitkat, imploring them to help him.

I wish I could, thought Ben. But what can I do? How can the four of us get past four of them?

And if we don't – if we stay here, stuck in this small room – what are they going to do to us?

A minute later, all his questions were answered.

46

The Tiger stepped past the Scotsman and gave them a big, beaming smile. "Welcome, my sons and my daughters. Welcome to my house."

Apart from his shining eyes, he was an unimpressive figure with short arms and short legs and a little pot belly bulging under his long yellow robe.

"Tell me something," said the Tiger. "What are you doing here? Have you come to find someone?"

The Scotsman stepped forward. "He said he was—"

"Let them speak," said the Tiger. "I want to hear from them, not from you." He turned to the Misfitz. "What are your names?"

None of them answered. They hadn't discussed what to do in this situation and none of them wanted to be the first to give away any important information.

The Tiger said, "If you don't want to tell me who you are, will you at least tell me what you are doing in my house?"

"We don't want to be here," said Ben. "You have no right to lock us up. We want to leave."

"You can leave," said the Tiger.

"Can we?"

"Anyone can leave at any time. No one is holding you here against your will."

"We can walk out right now?"

"Of course."

"Great," said Ben. "We'd like to go now, please."

"I don't want to go anywhere," said Frank. "I want to see my mother."

"Who is your mother?" said the Tiger.

"Nina Fitzroy," said Frank. "You know her as Padma. She was given that name at an ashram in Kerala."

"Padma is your mother?"

"Yes."

"You are lucky," said the Tiger. "No son could ask for a better mother. She is a very wise woman."

"I want to see her," said Frank.

"Padma has joined us on a silent retreat. She is meditating and fasting. She has taken a vow of silence and a vow of solitude. She does not wish to see anyone."

"She'll want to see me," said Frank.

"Of course she will. When her retreat is finished and she emerges into the world. But not till then."

"You're lying," cried Frank. "You've kidnapped her! Let me see her!"

"She is here because she wants to be here," said the Tiger. "She was searching for the truth and now she has found the truth. She is happy, my child. And you should be happy for her happiness."

"Liar! Let me see my mum! Let her go!"

"Do you want to see proof?"

"Proof? What proof?"

"I will show you."

The Tiger beckoned to one of his assistants and spoke to him in a low tone. The assistant nodded and hurried away.

They waited for a minute or two in silence. Frank paced back and forth. Ben studied the Tiger's face, looking at his fierce brown eyes and his benevolent smile, wondering who he really was and what he was doing here. How had he managed to persuade forty men and women to come and live with him in this big house? Did he drug them? Or con them? Or were they really here because they wanted to be? And if so, why?

The assistant returned with a sheet of paper. The Tiger glanced at it, then handed it to Frank. "Tell me, is this your mother's signature?"

Frank read the short handwritten statement. The others gathered round and read it too.

I, NINA FITZROY, request to spend
FOURTEEN DAYS on a silent retreat at
Montgomery House. For that time, I do not
want any contact with the world, no matter
what happens.
Signed
Nina Fitzroy

"You see?" said the Tiger. "Am I lying to you?"

"No," said Frank. "You're telling the truth. This is my mother's writing."

"You see the date?"

"Yes."

The document was dated the day that Nina had disappeared.

"Fourteen days," said the Tiger. "That is her specific request. During that time, she does not wish to be disturbed. This is a necessity for the good progress of the silent retreat."

"My mother had an accident." Frank spoke in a quiet, determined voice. He had been passionate and angry before, but now he sounded entirely calm and rational. "She was cycling to work and she was knocked off her bike. She hit her head. An ambulance came. They took her to hospital. That's where you met her, isn't it?"

The Tiger nodded. "Arthur cut himself. We took him to hospital to be healed. We met Padma in the waiting room and she asked to come with us."

"She hadn't been seen by the doctors," said Frank.

"She told us she was not ill. She said she wished to join us."

"She didn't know what she was doing," said Frank. "She hit her head. She might have concussion or amnesia. Her brain could be damaged. Yes, this is her signature, but it doesn't matter. She needs to go back to the hospital and see a doctor."

"I have to respect her wishes," said the Tiger. "She wants to be here."

"If she wanted to be here, why wouldn't she tell anyone what she was doing?"

"Did she not tell you?" The Tiger looked surprised. "She asked to send a postcard. We posted it for her. Was that not for you?"

"Yes, but..."

"But what?"

Frank thought for a moment. Then he said, "Won't you just let me talk to her?"

"It is not possible," said the Tiger. "She has asked to join a silent retreat for two weeks. For that time, conversation is strictly forbidden. I can understand why you wish to see your mother, but you must respect her own wishes. You cannot talk to her."

Frank said, "What if I talk to her without her talking back?"

47

Nina was overjoyed to see her son, but she didn't say a word. She just hurled her arms around him, squeezing him in a tight hug.

She held him for a long time. Then she stepped back and looked at him. Her brows were furrowed.

Frank said, "Hello, Mum."

Nina looked at Ben and Harmony and Kitkat, then back at Frank. He was waiting for her to speak, but she didn't say a word.

"This is crazy," said Frank. "Can't you talk to me? Why do you have to keep this stupid vow?"

Nina looked at the Tiger.

He seemed to know exactly what she meant.

"You may write," he said. "I have decided to make an exception. In this case, writing is not breaking silence."

He gestured at one of his assistants, who hurried forward with a pencil and a notepad.

Nina wrote fast, then turned the pad to face Frank.

I thought I heard you. During meditation. Was that your voice?

"Yes," said Frank. "That was me."

Nina smiled. She scribbled again:

I thought I was hallucinating! It's so lovely to see you, Frank. But what are you doing here?

"I've come to get you."

Where's Jeremy?

"In London."

Does he know you're here?

"No."

I don't understand. How did you get here?

"Mum, where do you think you are?"

In the ashram.

"Where is the ashram?"

Here.

"Which country are you in?'

Silly question!

"Just answer it, Mum. What country are you in?"

She wrote the answer in big letters, then turned the paper to face him.

India.

48

For a moment, no one spoke. They stared at the five letters in silence. Then the Tiger said, "Padma, look at me."

Nina lifted her head and stared into his hypnotic eyes.

"I have made a mistake," said the Tiger. His voice was quiet and melancholy. "I should not have brought you here."

Nina reached for the paper and the pen, but the Tiger pushed them away.

"You are released," he said. "Your retreat is finished. You may speak. You *must* speak." He had the sheet of paper that she had signed. He tore it in half. "You are released from the retreat, Padma, and all its obligations. You must leave here right now."

Nina had not spoken for many days and her first word was so quiet that the others could barely hear her. She whispered, "Why?"

"I was wrong, Padma," said the Tiger. "I should have left you in the hospital. Now you must leave the Ashram and go with your son. He will take you back there."

"Back where?"

"To the hospital."

"I don't understand. Which hospital?"

Frank put his hand on his mother's arm. "Mum, you're not in India."

Nina laughed out loud. Then she realized Frank was serious and the smile faded from her face. "Where am I?"

"We're in Abbots Leigh. On the other side of the Clifton Bridge. We can get home in fifteen minutes."

"That's ridiculous. That's impossible."

"You had an accident. You hit your head. You've been missing for a week. The police have been looking for you. So have we."

Nina looked at Harmony, Kitkat and Ben. Then she looked at the Tiger. "Is this true?"

"Yes, Padma. This is all true."

Nina turned to her son. She put her hands on his shoulders. "Oh, Frank. I'm so sorry."

"Don't worry, Mum. It's not your fault."

"I'm still so very sorry. Now, will you take me home?"

49

Ben rang Konrad and asked him to collect them.

Frank went upstairs with his mother and gathered her possessions from the dormitory, which she shared with five other women. She changed out of her yellow robe and back into her own clothes.

Frank searched her red rucksack. He found her phone. The screen was cracked. The phone was dead. It must have been smashed in the accident and not worked since.

This time, when the white van stopped at the gates to Montgomery House, they were opened immediately. Konrad drove up the gravel drive and parked outside the house.

Nina spent a long time saying goodbye to everyone. Frank and the others waited impatiently by the van. They wanted to get out of here as quickly as possible, but Nina refused to be rushed.

Just as they were finally ready to leave, the tall, skinny Scotsman walked out of the house, carrying four necklaces looped over his right arm. They were the same necklaces that Nina, the Scotsman and everyone else were wearing over their yellow robes: a narrow black cord strung with two brown gems. The Scotsman took them to the Tiger, who gathered Nina and the Misfitz.

"I want to give you a gift," said the Tiger. "This is to say thank you for coming here. And also to say how much I admire your courage and your commitment. Not all children would do so much for their mother. You must love her very, very much." He smiled benevolently at Frank and Nina and the others. Then he reached for the necklaces. "I have a small gift for each of you. Nothing more than a token of my appreciation. This is what I give to all my children." He cupped the gems in his palm. "These are my eyes."

"Yuck," said Kitkat.

The Tiger smiled. "You need not worry, my daughter. They are not really my eyes. They are two precious jewels, all the way from India. I call them my eyes because they are blessed by me. I give them a special power. If you wear them round your neck, they will watch over you. Wear them every day. Wherever you are, I will be there too. I will be your guide. I will protect you and watch over you. Will you do that for me? Will you wear this necklace every day?"

Kitkat nodded. "Sure."

Ben said, "I don't know if I can wear it to school."

"Of course you can," said the Tiger. "You must wear it every day. Wherever you go, whatever you do, I will be there too."

He took one of the necklaces from the Scotsman's arm and hung it around Kitkat's neck, then clasped his hands together in front of his chest and said, "Peace be with you."

"Peace be," echoed the forty men and women who were clustered around them, watching the ceremony.

"Thank you very much," said Kitkat, fingering the two brown gems. "They're lovely."

The Tiger repeated the same gesture three more times, hanging a necklace around the necks of Ben, Harmony and Frank.

"Peace be with you," he said to each of them.

"Peace be," repeated his followers.

"Thanks," said Ben.

"Thank you," said Harmony.

Frank said nothing.

They climbed into the van and drove out of Montgomery House.

Frank and Nina sat in the front with Konrad. Ben, Harmony and Kitkat squatted on the floor in the back.

They drove up the lane, down the hill, past the pub and the shop, and over Clifton Bridge.

When they reached the Bristol side of the bridge, Frank asked Konrad to stop the van.

"What is problem?" said Konrad.

"There's no problem," said Frank. "I just have to get out for a second."

"Is double yellow line. I will get ticket. We can stop later."

"Please stop here," insisted Frank.

Konrad sighed. He bumped the van up on to the pavement and parked illegally, then opened the doors and let everyone out. They stood on the grassy verge, staring at Frank, wondering why he was so desperate to stop and get out.

Frank was still wearing the string of beads that he had been given by the Tiger. He lifted them over his neck and held them in his right hand. Then he pointed at Kitkat's. "Can I have those?"

"Why do you want them?"

"Please, just give them to me."

"Tell me why and I will."

"Come on, Kitkat. Hand them over."

Kitkat reluctantly lifted the beads over her neck and handed them to her brother.

Frank collected the strings of beads from Ben, Harmony and his mother too. Then he walked back to the bridge, lifted the five strings over his head and swung them like a lasso.

The beads spun through the air at the end of his outstretched arm.

Back and forth.

Faster and faster.

Frank let go.

The beads and the black cord whirled across the parapet and disappeared over the edge of the bridge.

50

Two doctors came to look at Nina.

The first inspected her head and asked how she was feeling. Did she have headaches? Or pains in her back or neck? Had she been sleeping well?

Nina said she felt fine and would like to go home.

The second was more interested in her mind. He produced a sheaf of photos and asked her to identify the famous faces: Robert de Niro, Michelle Obama, Roger Federer, Miley Cyrus, David Beckham, Grace Kelly, John Wayne, Leona Lewis, Jack Straw, Paris Hilton and all kinds of other men and women, old and young, recent and ancient, famous and forgotten.

Nina recognized more than Frank, but fewer than Kitkat.

When Nina had been through the photos, the doctor asked a long list of questions, writing down her answers on a clipboard. He wanted to know her name, her address, the names of her parents, the names of her grandparents, the names of her next-door neighbours, what she had eaten for breakfast, what she had eaten for supper last night, today's date, the year, the name of the prime minister, the capital of France and the last place that she'd been on holiday. She answered every question correctly.

The doctor led Frank into the corridor and talked to him in a low voice.

"As far as we can tell, your mother is suffering from concussion combined with retrograde amnesia. Do you know what that means?"

"I know what amnesia is," said Frank. "But what's retrograde?"

"Amnesia simply means a loss of memory," said the doctor. "We divide it into retrograde and anterograde. When a patient suffers from retrograde amnesia, he or she can't remember events that occurred before the onset of the memory loss. In other words, your mother's brain is now working normally in most respects. She can retain information. If you tell her something, she won't forget it. If you met her for the first time, you wouldn't even notice that there was anything wrong. She knows where she is. She knows the date, the time and the name of the prime minister. But she can't remember her accident and she's still confused about events both before and after it."

"You're saying the crash destroyed her memory?"

"'Destroyed' is a strong word. I would prefer 'disrupted'. She temporarily lost her memory of the past few months and believed she was back in India."

"But how could that happen?"

"Amnesia can have different causes," said the doctor. "Some are psychological. If you experience a terrible event – a car crash, for instance – you may be unable to remember what happened to you. Your brain blocks out the memories of the traumatic event. Do you understand?"

"You mean my mum can't remember what happened to her because it was so horrible?"

"That's one possible explanation. However, in this case, I believe that the cause of the amnesia is physical rather than psychological. Your mother hurt her head. The brain has been damaged. That sounds bad, but it needn't be. We're not yet sure exactly which parts of her brain have suffered the most damage, nor how much of this damage is going to be permanent, but I should imagine, simply from my initial observation of her symptoms, your mother is going to be fine."

"Can she come home?"

"Not yet. We're going to keep her in hospital and do some more tests. We should be able to give you a much more secure diagnosis in a couple of days."

51

They knew they had to confess everything to Jennifer and Jeremy. There was only one thing to decide: who would do the talking.

No one wanted to.

Frank kept out of the whole conversation. He wasn't interested. He just wanted to stay with his mother. He sat in the room with her while the others went into the corridor to argue it out.

Each of them came up with all sorts of reasons why they were the wrong person to make the call, but they couldn't reach an agreement. Finally they put it to a vote.

Ben said, "Who votes for Harmony?"

He was the only one to raise his hand.

He said, "Who votes for Kitkat?"

No one did.

Ben sighed. He could see where this was going. "Go on, then. Who votes for me?"

Harmony and Kitkat raised their right hands.

Two against one.

"That's not fair," said Ben. "You're ganging up on me because you're girls and I'm a boy."

"Life isn't fair," said Harmony.

"Oh, great. Now you're turning into Mum."

Ben rang his mother.

"Where are you?" said Jennifer. "What's going on? Why aren't you answering your phones? I rang your schools. I rang your friends. I rang the Lancasters and Kurkovs. I rang Granny and Grandpa. I rang everyone I could think of. I was just about to ring the police. Where are you?"

"You don't have to worry about us," said Ben. "We're fine."

"But where are you?"

"The thing is, Mum, I've got some great news. You're going to be so happy. We found Frank's mum."

"You've found Nina?"

"Yes."

"How amazing. That's wonderful. How did you find her?"

Ben started explaining what had happened. He hadn't said more than a few words when Jennifer interrupted him.

"Wait a minute," she said. "Do you mean you went to Bristol?"

"We had to. Otherwise we wouldn't have found her."

"*We?* All four of you?"

"Yes."

"Including Kitkat?"

"Yes."

"But. . . This doesn't. . . I don't. . ." Jennifer took a deep breath. "Where are you now?"

"In hospital. Don't worry, nothing's happened to us. We're here with Frank's mum. The nurses are looking after her."

"What's the name of the hospital?"

Jennifer jumped in the car and went to pick up Jeremy. Then they drove to Bristol together.

While Jeremy was driving, Jennifer rang Ben and Harmony's father.

He answered immediately. "Hello?"

"Hello, Robert. It's me."

"Me? Who's me?"

"Your ex-wife."

"Oh, that me. Hello, Jennifer. I'm actually in a meeting. Can this wait?"

"No, it can't," said Jennifer.

She told him what the kids had done.

"It's a great story," said Robert. "I'm going to mention it to a couple of writers. We could turn it into a wonderful movie."

"That's not funny," said Jennifer.

"It's not meant to be," said Robert. "I'm completely serious. There's only one problem. What happens at the end? Does she get better? Or is she going to stay crazy for ever?"

"I knew I shouldn't have rung you."

"No, no. It's good you told me. You should tell me everything. I want to be involved with my children's welfare."

"Involved? You're six thousand miles away and you haven't seen them for almost a year. How can you call that 'involved'?"

"I see them as often as I can."

"Hah!"

"I'm taking them to Morocco, aren't I?"

"Are you? Really? Or will you cancel at the last moment like you did last time?"

"That's not fair," said Robert. "You know I couldn't say no to Brad."

Jennifer didn't bother arguing with her ex-husband. She had argued with him enough over the years, both during and after their marriage, and she had learnt one useful lesson: Robert would never, ever admit that he was wrong. She said goodbye, put the phone down and turned to her husband. "What are we going to do with them?"

"Who?"

"Our impossible children! How are we going to punish them this time?"

"We're not," said Jeremy.

"Why not?"

"Because they found Nina. They shouldn't have gone to Bristol. But they did and they found her. And nothing else really matters."

52

There was a new sign pinned to Ben's bedroom door.

The old one had been taken down, rolled up, tied with an elastic band and hidden under a chest of drawers.

The new one said:

KEEP OUT!!!!!
THIS IS PRIVATE PROPERTY
TRESPASSERS WILL BE PERSECUTED
By order of
Benjamin Amis and Frank Fitzroy

The sign would stay on the door for fourteen days and then the old one would be unrolled and put up again.

The doctors didn't want Nina to go straight home. Her memory appeared to be working properly. Her brain hadn't suffered any permanent damage. She could look after herself. Despite all these positive signs, they didn't want to take any chances and so they asked her to stay in the hospital for another fortnight. This time, she did as she was told.

Frank would go back to Bristol as soon she was released.

A fortnight was fine, Ben had decided. A month would be impossible. Three weeks would be unbearable. But he didn't mind sharing his room for another fourteen days.

Ben kept his pens in a jam jar on his desk. He picked out a newly sharpened pencil and offered it to Frank.

"Do you want to do it?" he said. "Or shall I?"

"You can," said Frank.

"Are you sure?"

"Yup. I trust you."

Ben knelt on the floor at the far end of the room. He had already marked out the correct positions, one midway along each wall, and strung a long wire between them, giving himself a guide.

He put the tip of his pencil to the floor and drew a line from one wall to the other, cutting the room in half.

Everything to the north of that line belonged to Ben.

Everything to the south belonged to Frank.

As soon as the line was drawn, Ben and Frank grabbed their possessions and hauled them to their side of the line.

Books, pens, plants, computers, socks, shoes, pants, jumpers – everything had to be moved.

From midnight tonight, their territories would be strictly separated and they would forfeit any possessions which were found on the wrong side of the line.

The warm kitchen was full of good smells. Harmony opened the oven and drew out a freshly baked chocolate cake.

"That looks yummy," said Kitkat.

"Don't touch! It's hot."

"I know, I know. I'm just looking. And smelling. Hmmmm."

Kitkat followed the chocolate cake to the kitchen table, drawing deep draughts of its delicious scent. She had already made the icing, following strict instructions from her elder sister, and now she was going to plaster it over the cake.

There were two types of icing.

One was white, flavoured with vanilla, and the other was brown, coloured with cocoa powder.

They waited for the cake to cool down, then applied the first coat, the brown one, covering the cake's sides and top with a smooth layer of chocolate icing.

They left it to set. Harmony did the washing-up. Kitkat dried and put away.

When the chocolate icing had hardened, Harmony squeezed some of the vanilla icing into a tube and handed it to Kitkat.

"All yours," she said. "Good luck."

Kitkat knelt on a chair and hunched over the cake. Working very slowly, taking great care not to make any mistakes, she wrote seven wonky letters in white icing.

m i s f i t z

When Kitkat finished the final "z", she put the tube on the table, dipped her finger into the bowl and scraped out a large, dribbly scoop.

Harmony said, "You're not supposed to. . ."

But it was too late. Kitkat had already put her finger in her mouth. She sucked it clean and pulled it out with a loud pop. "Yum, yum, yum,

yum, yum! That is delicious! Can I have a piece of cake?"

"Not yet."

"Just a tiny little taste," begged Kitkat.

"Go and get the boys," said Harmony. "We should eat this together."

Kitkat didn't need telling twice. She jumped off the chair and bolted up the stairs.

a **MISFITZ** mystery

The
One That Got Away

JOSH LACEY

Quarryman's Cottage –
the perfect holiday hideaway

The perfect place to die of boredom! Ben is stuck there for the summer with his sister, half-sister and Freaky Frank, his weird stepbrother. They're driving him nuts. Then the thief strikes…

What kind of burglar picks all the strawberries in the dead of night? The four Misfitz uncover even stranger secrets when they follow the trail into the forbidden quarry…

Turn the page to read the first chapter!

1

Ben was woken at 5.25 in the morning. He shoved his hand under the pillow and felt for his phone. He'd set it on silent, so the alarm vibrated through the pillow, interrupting his sleep without making any noise.

He pressed a key to switch it off.

He sat up slowly and peered over the edge of his bed, looking down at the bottom bunk. There was a lump under the duvet. It didn't move. It carried on not moving. Frank was still asleep.

Dawn wasn't for another ten minutes, but slim chinks of light were already sneaking through the curtains. Ben knew he didn't have any time to waste. If he was going to catch the thief, he had to do it now.

He pushed aside the duvet, slid out of bed and

climbed down the ladder, trying not to make any noise.

The floorboards felt cold against his bare feet.

Ben had slept in his T-shirt and boxer shorts, ready for an early start, and left his jeans, socks and trainers in a neat pile on a chair. He bundled them into his arms and tiptoed across the room. Dressing downstairs would make much less noise. He opened the door, glanced once more at Frank, checking he hadn't woken up, then went into the corridor.

He closed the door behind him and listened for a few seconds.

If his mum or his sisters had woken up, he would have heard their voices or their footsteps, but the house was quiet. They were still asleep.

Ben padded along the corridor and down the stairs. In the hallway, he pulled on his clothes, then crouched on the icy flagstones to tie up his shoes.

He opened the front door. The cold air grabbed the bare skin of his face and arms. He should have worn a jumper. Too late now. Maybe the air would warm up when the sun rose.

Pulling the door shut behind him, he walked into the front garden and had a pee against the stone wall. He hadn't wanted to use the loo upstairs in case the noise woke anyone.

Birds flitted between the trees that surrounded the cottage. In the sky, a few wispy clouds were catching the first rays of the rising sun. Ben didn't often take much notice of nature, but this was beautiful. He should have brought a camera.

No time to worry about that now.

He walked round the side of the cottage, opened the gate and went into the vegetable garden.

There was no one to be seen. The garden looked the same as yesterday. Nothing had been disturbed.

Ben walked to a patch of grass at the far end of the garden and sat down. It was the perfect spot. As soon as someone came into the garden, he would see them.

He might have to hang around for an hour. Maybe even two. But he didn't mind. He'd stay all day if he had to.

He leaned back against the fence and settled down for a long wait.

When he opened his eyes, the sun had risen above the trees.

Hours must have passed. He had fallen asleep.

I'm an idiot, thought Ben. What kind of detective falls asleep in the middle of a stake-out?

Someone could have come and taken everything and he wouldn't even have noticed.

He sat up and looked around, checking to see if anything had changed.

That was when he saw the thief.